BARRACK ONE

ELYSE HOFFMAN

ISBN 978-1-952742-04-0 (ebook)

Project 613 Publishing
Project613Publishing.com

PROJECT613

*Dedicated to my mother and father for their enduring
support
To my grandfather whose stories I never heard
To all of the children whose futures were stolen by the
Nazi Regime
And to God, Who makes all stories*

BARRACK ONE

"Vilém, we need to talk..."

"We probably do, but can we do it after *this asshole quits tailing me?!*"

Jana snickered and craned her neck to look behind her. They were on their way to visit Vilém's parents—since they were planning on having their wedding in Prague and Tomas Rehor had offered to pay for the ceremony, they had to go over all of their plans.

Jana was just hoping her fiancé would be able to get them there in one piece. Unfortunately, Vilém refused to let Jana go anywhere near the wheel while she was pregnant, insisting that she sit shotgun and hug a pillow to her chest while he drove. Which normally wouldn't have been a problem, but even though it had been weeks since the spirit of Kommandant Gerber had injured his eyes, Vilém's vision still hadn't fully recovered.

"Vil, he's not tailing us, you're blind," Jana sighed.

"He is *directly* on my butt! If he was any closer, I'd have to ask *him* to marry me," Vilém said with a smirk.

"Vilém!" laughed Jana, slapping his arm.

"Fuck it, I'm pulling over. Let's get something to eat and let this guy pass," Vilém suggested. He found a drive-thru and joined the line.

"Oh, come on!" Vilém cried as the driver behind him, evidently famished, followed him off the road. Jana shoved her face into her mandatory pillow in a desperate attempt to protect Vilém's pride as she laughed herself stupid.

"Oh, yes, laugh! Laugh at my misery!" Vilém teased. "All right, well, we're stuck between an indecisive orderer and a literal ass-kisser, so I guess we might as well talk."

"Okay..." Jana sighed, setting her pillow back in her lap and grabbing her fiancé's hand. "Listen, Vil...the Camp, I know it's a good job with good pay, and I know you do wonderful work there..."

"Oh, don't tell me you want me to quit!" Vilém cried, trying to achieve a joking tone but unable to stop genuine disappointment from slipping into his voice. "Ms. Doubek's finally bearable! She actually likes me now!"

"I know, honey," Jana said, tugging his hand towards her belly. "But I'm thinking about the baby and...I don't wanna have to raise her alone because some crazy Nazi ghost killed her daddy. I know you still wanna get rid of the Kommandant, but..."

"Jana," Vilém sighed, gently patting her stomach. "I'm thinking about the baby too, you know I am. If he can hurt me, he could hurt someone else...he could hurt her someday. I'm not gonna let her grow up with the same worries your grandma had."

"She's gonna be a Jew, Vilém. Ghost or no ghost, she's gonna have to grow up with some of those worries. You can't stop that."

"I can mitigate it. Look, nobody else has been able to see or hear Gerber or any other ghost. I've gotten rid of the last four..."

"They were good people, though. They weren't Nazis."

"Sweetie, Klammer," Vilém reminded her, and she threw up her hands.

"Fine, one ex-Nazi! Same difference! Oh, I'm just so worried...if he can hurt your eyes this bad..."

"Then he's gotta go," Vilém said. "He may be a Nazi, but he's still human. If I can figure out why he's still here, maybe I can force him to give it up and get out."

"Maybe. But for all you know, his unfinished business may be that he didn't kill enough Jews. Him and Heydrich are probably just angry the Final Solution wasn't final."

Vilém's eyes widened, but he didn't dare say a word. Heydrich! He had almost forgotten that the Hangman of Prague's ghost was almost certainly still lingering in Prague. Information on Kommandant Gerber had been nearly impossible to come by even with Ms. Doubek's enthusiastic assistance, but Kommandant Gerber and Heydrich *had* been "friends."

Perhaps the Blonde Beast could give him something besides grief for once.

3

The soon-to-be-newlyweds arrived at the Rehor residence in somewhat decent time despite Vilém's road rage almost leading to an all-out brawl ("Vilém, I can't believe you said that to him, you're lucky he didn't kill you!" "Maybe next time he won't sexually harass my car!")

Vilém hadn't even put the car in park when his mother appeared outside Jana's door. Squealing, Lida Rehor pulled her almost-daughter-in-law out of the vehicle and into an embrace so crushing that Jana was almost afraid for her baby.

"Hiya, Mrs. Rehor!" she cried.

"Oh, *stop*, you! When will you learn?" cried Lida, kissing Jana's cheek.

"My bad, Mama Lida!" giggled Jana, returning the greeting and pecking her future mother-in-law's cheek. Vilém stumbled out of the car and Tomas, showing much more enthusiasm than he normally would, darted from the porch and pulled his son into a half-hug.

"There he is!" laughed Tomas. Vilém grinned and teasingly shoved his father away.

"Hey, what kinda trick is this?" he cried.

"No tricks! I just love you!" Tomas decreed, ruffling Vilém's hair. Vilém pursed his lips together with derisive suspicion.

"Plus, I have to stay on your good side," Tomas joked. "You're about to give me my first grandchild, so for once I have to pretend you're the favorite!"

"Aha! I knew there was a twist!" Vilém cried,

wagging an accusatory finger in his father's face. Lida and Tomas helped the couple take their bags into the house.

"Since you're going to be newlyweds, you two can share the same room now!" Lida declared, lifting Jana's hefty suitcase up to Vilém's old bedroom.

"It's not a sin anymore," Tomas chuckled.

"I think the real sin is asking us to share a twin bed," Vilém snickered, and Jana patted her stomach.

"Only room for two! Sorry, sweetie, you're on the floor," she declared.

"I'm sleeping down here with the cactuses," Vilém joked. He looked around at the menagerie of cacti that decorated his parents' living room, sparing a glance at the picture of his grinning Grandpa Fabian that rested among the plants. The cactuses always reminded him of his grandfather's less-than-green thumb and all the hours they had spent together, painting pots for the succulents.

His eyes flitted to the top of the TV and he was surprised to see a familiar plant sitting in a pot decorated with tiger stripes. The name 'STEVE' was painted on the rim.

"Mama, I thought Steve died!" he cried, stepping close to the imposter cactus and scowling down at it, realizing that although from the distance it was a dead-ringer for Steve, up close it looked subtly different.

"Oh, honey, I know, but Oda loves Steve and she's going to be down here for the wedding!" Lida cried from upstairs.

"Mamaaaa, that's pretty deceptive! There's only one

Steve!" Vilém proclaimed, crossing his arms and glowering at Not-Steve. "Steve is irreplaceable."

"I wish I could have met Steve," Jana sighed wistfully, shaking her head and hugging her belly. "The baby could have used a godfather!"

"Hey, you said no godfathers! I already told Erik no!" Vilém laughed. "I mean, granted, Steve still would have been a better godfather than Erik..."

"Vil-Vil, if you're really upset, we can call that one Steve Junior," Lida said, trotting down the stairs and grabbing a sharpie from a nearby desk, tossing it to her son. Vilém nodded and drew a large, prominent "JR" next to the "STEVE."

"I guess Oda has to learn about death eventually," sighed Lida.

"Mama...Oda's twenty," Vilém pointed out.

"She's still my baby and so are you!" Lida cried, pinching her son's cheek. "Oh, speaking of babies...Jana! Come, me and Tomas went shopping and we bought the most adorable clothes for the baby! We kept everything purple, nice and gender-neutral."

Vilém followed his wife-to-be and mother into Emma's room, which was packed to the brim with purple baby clothes, toys, and even a cradle. He hung back, letting Jana and his mother have their fun, until he felt a tap on his shoulder.

"All joking aside," Tomas whispered in his son's ear. "I'm very proud of you!"

"Of what, Old Man?" snickered Vilém. "Jana's the one who's doing all the work!"

"I can see that look in your eyes. Same look I had

when we were about to have you. You're stressed, and that's good! It means you're worried, and it means you're going to try your hardest. You grew into a good man and you're going to be an excellent father. I'm proud of you. And don't worry too much about the baby..."

"Pap, the baby may be the least of my worries right now," Vilém sighed.

Vilém did his best to keep Jana and his parents awake for as long as possible. He wanted them to sleep deeply. By 2 AM, everyone in the house was practically dead. He slipped into his old bedroom and kissed his snoozing fiancée's forehead.

"Don't freak out," he whispered. He tiptoed out of the room and down the stairs, pausing to smile affectionately at Fabian before darting out of the house and rushing to the car.

It probably would have been dangerous for anyone else to drive when they were as sleep-deprived as Vilém, but he was so used to adjusting and readjusting his sleep schedule that he managed a relatively lengthy drive without so much as a droopy eyelid.

He drove until he reached the corner of Kubišova Street. When Vilém had been young, there had been no memorial, but now a tall tower stood at the spot where two brave Czech partisans had assassinated the Butcher of Prague. Shaped like a triangle with three metal men poised at the top holding out their arms, as though they were preparing to take a bullet for their nation.

Vilém parked near the memorial. Thankfully, the street was practically vacant at this early hour and only a few cars whizzed by. He hopped out of his car and approached the triangular tower, looking down at the flickering candles and vibrant flowers that grateful Czechs had left for the partisans.

"Well, he wouldn't be here..." Vilém muttered. He tried to remember where he had been standing when he had previously sensed Heydrich's spirit. He marched around, keeping his eyes as close to shut as possible without rendering himself blind. The last thing he wanted was to bumble right into traffic. He imagined Heydrich would find that amusing.

Vilém trudged through the trimmed grass until a freezing breeze struck him. He shuddered and opened his eyes, looking under his foot and realizing that there was a small triangle-shaped boulder jutting out of the dirt. He initially couldn't see why Heydrich would choose to cling to a tiny rock of all things, but he glanced from the boulder to the statue and chuckled when he realized what the Nazi's thought process must have been.

"Jealous asshole..." he whispered. Heydrich had chosen a rejected scrap from the memorial.

Vilém knelt down and rubbed his hands together. "All right, let's see if this works for evil ghosts."

He shut his eyes and pressed his hand against the tiny triangle.

"Hey, Reichsprotektor," he greeted the Nazi. A small wave of aggravation crashed against him.

Go away. Vilém recognized the squeaky voice right away. Definitely Heydrich.

"So what's keeping you here, Heydrich? Didn't burn enough babies to death?"

I have nothing to say to you.

"You don't seem to be very busy."

How did you see me?

"I followed the trail of blood," Vilém grumbled. "Listen, this isn't pleasant for me either, but I'm willing to trade information for information. I want info on Kommandant Hans Gerber. You give that to me, I'll give you something."

You don't have anything to offer me. We lost. That's all. I don't care about anything out there.

"Not even Klaus?" Vilém hissed, and he felt a small burst of sadness emanate from Heydrich's spirit at hearing the name of his beloved son.

No. No I do not.

"That's a lie. You're a monster, but not *that* much of a monster."

I'm not a monster. There's nothing you can tell me about Klaus. He's dead. He's gone.

"So what are you still doing here? I was kidding about the not enough burned babies thing, but..."

You're not even a real person! Heydrich's spirit had evidently had enough small-talk and sarcasm. Vilém winced as he felt a sharp pain in his hand, as though someone had dug their fingernails into his flesh. He grunted. Intimidation? Well, Vilém wasn't about to run away.

He sat silently for a moment, gritting his teeth, his skin screaming for him to hurry up and think of something. Threatening a ghost wouldn't work, but he remembered reading about the Hangman's Achilles' Heel.

"Wow...you're really pathetic..." said Vilém, letting a

grin take over his face. He suppressed a yelp of pain as the Nazi ghost punched his hand.

"Is *that* the best you've got?" Vilém giggled.

You're a very stupid Czech...

But Heydrich's ghost fell silent as Vilém started laughing, laughing as though he had heard the greatest joke in the universe, laughing so hard it hurt worse than anything the dead Nazi could do to him.

What...what's so funny?

"You, Billy-Goat! You and that voice, you sound like a lamb!"

I....

"And what are you doing right now? Stepping on my hand? Oh, how the mighty have fallen! What am I saying? You were never mighty! I heard your mom used to beat the shit outta you when you were a kid."

Enough...

"Did Mommy make you cry, Reini? Did Mommy say she didn't love you, so you decided to take it out on some helpless people? Did that make you feel big, Reini? Did killing Jews make you feel better about yourself, Reini?"

Enough, I said!

"Did it make you feel like a hero, Reini? Klaus said he thought you were a hero! Remember his face when he found out your secret? Oh, he was so disappointed. He thought you were a hero, and then he thought you were a monster. Oh, poor kid didn't even know! You're not a monster, you're just a pathetic little nobody. A dumb little goat that wanted to be a wolf. Bleat more, come on! Baaa! Baaa!"

Enough, enough, enough! Stop talking! Shut your mouth and don't talk about my son!

Heydrich's ghost attacked Vilém's hand, and Vilém could feel his fingers crack. But he kept laughing. He laughed and laughed and the ghost's anger morphed into desperation.

Stop laughing at me!

"Jesus, don't tell me anything about Gerber! I want an excuse to stay here and listen to you squeak! It's so funny!"

I'm not funny! I bathed the streets of Prague in Czech blood, I...

"'I bathed the streets of Prague in Czech Blood', ha!" Vilém cried, making his voice absurdly high-pitched as he teased the Blonde Beast.

Oh, you're as bad as...you know what? I'll tell you whatever you want to know about Gerber if you promise to leave me alone and never come here again!

"Not a problem, Reini," Vilém snickered, letting his raucous laughter fade. "I don't want to save your soul."

That seems to be a common sentiment around here...all right, you wanted to know about Gerber. What about him?

"His ghost is still at the Camp, and he's being a nuisance."

That sounds like Hans.

"I heard you two were friends."

I don't have any friends.

"Golly, I wonder why! You're so pleasant. All I wanna know is why he may still be there and how I could convince him to leave...short of 'finish the Holocaust.'"

I don't think you'll have to worry about that. Gerber was a National Socialist, but nowhere near as ardent as most. He never would have gotten as far in the Party as he did were it not for my kindness.

"His favorite hobby was taking pictures of dead Jews, how was he not 'ardent'?"

Oh, he hated Jews. More than me, actually. He hated everything about Judaism. But he had his...strayings.

"Not like you, you never strayed."

Czech, you should learn this: there was never a perfect National Socialist.

"Himmler and Hitler called *you* the perfect Nazi after you died."

Ha! Now that...that is funny. I'm sure Goebbels wrote a lovely script for my funeral...well, you don't care about me.

"Nobody does."

Yes...well, Gerber, then. He hated Jews for personal reasons. His father served in the First World War, Martin Gerber...

"Martin?" Vilém cried. "Martin was his...well, his so-called son's name, the name of the Jewish child he kidnapped..."

What?

"Guess he kept this from you...there was this little blonde Jewish kid, Gerber stole him from his parents and was trying to make him become 'Aryan.'"

I know exactly who you're talking about. Gerber and his lies—he told me the boy was his illegitimate child. But...Jews can't become Aryan. Are you sure the child wasn't a mischling?

"A what?"

Part-Jew, mixed race. If the boy only had one Jewish grandparent or one Jewish parent...well, depending on how liberal Gerber became while I wasn't looking, he could have decided the boy wasn't a real Jew. The definition of "Jew" tended to vary from person to person in the Reich. Goering used to say he would decide who was Jewish, but even with the Nuremberg Laws, a lot of it became a matter of guesswork and preference.

"These rules seem arbitrary and stupid."

This isn't a debate, Czech. The point is: it doesn't make sense for Gerber to take in a random Jew...he must have known something about the boy.

"Such as...?"

Perhaps the boy's father. I was just about to talk about that. Gerber's father died in the Great War...er...the first one...not the one I was in, the one before that...

"World War One. I get it. What happened?"

He gave his gas mask to a young child, a Jew. Gave his life for a little Jew.

"Jesus, you're lying..."

I'm not. I don't know many of the details, but Gerber said that the Jew his father saved lived in his house throughout his childhood. Evidently the Jew was a nightmare, constantly in trouble...I believe his name was Isaac Goldstein. The details are really not important. Use what few brain cells you have, Czech: clearly the Jewish child Gerber "adopted" wasn't just an experiment. Perhaps he was the son of Isaac, and if so, he would have possessed sentimental value. Gerber might have truly cared for him.

"Which would mean that when Little Martin ran

away from the Camp..." muttered Vilém. "That might be it...yeah..."

I said Gerber wasn't a truly ardent National Socialist for a reason: he cared less about his nation, less about the Cause, than he did about his own legacy. Everything he ever did was for his legacy. Our deeds are our legacy, but our children are as well. If he viewed Martin as a son, then the boy was his legacy.

"Legacy, hm...? Maybe he's not too happy with the legacy he has now. Maybe he wants a different legacy."

If you can communicate with me, you can communicate with Gerber. Bring up Isaac and his father, that should convince him to talk to you. Failing that, I suppose you could just annoy him into submission.

"If it comes to that," Vilém sneered. "So one more question before I leave, Heydrich: you said you weren't a perfect Nazi. If you're not still here because you're upset about not winning the war or killing all the Jews, why *are* you here?"

I have nowhere else to go.

"Too evil for Hell?"

Ha! I wish. Didn't you promise to leave me alone?

"Gladly. When you get the chance, please go to Hell..."

Already...

But Vilém removed his injured hand from the rock, refusing to let Heydrich have the last word. He stood up, hissed, and wiggled his fingers. Heydrich, even trying his hardest, hadn't broken Vilém's bones.

"Ha!" laughed Vilém, cradling his hand and glowering down at the little triangle. "You really *are* pathetic."

14

Vilém was lucky to be alive. Not because he had survived Heydrich's attack, but because Jana refrained from killing him when he called her from Bulovka Hospital. She took a taxi and stayed with him for the rest of the night. He was released by morning, and while Jana was merciful enough to spare his life, she was not merciful enough to leave his ears unharmed. Once they were away from the doctors and nurses, she started screaming at him and didn't stop until they pulled up to his parents' house.

"This is it, Vilém Rehor!" Jana shouted. "No more! You use the info Heydrich gave you! After that, no more! I can't do this..." She started to cry, clutching at her belly. He reached out and pulled her into an embrace.

"I know," he sighed. "I give. Just one try, and then nothing else."

"And if it looks like you'll get hurt..."

"I'll run," he promised, despising the notion of fleeing from a Nazi. Doing so would be a betrayal of his blood and pride, but Jana was right. He needed to stay safe for her, for his baby.

They spent the rest of the week with Lida and Tomas, planning the wedding and, in Vilém's case, coming up with increasingly stupid excuses for why his hand was bandaged ("I got attacked by lemurs on my way home from defending my fiancée's honor at the local distillery" quickly became Tomas' favorite). When the week ended and Vilém was obligated to go home, he insisted that Jana stay with his folks.

"I love Ilona, but if something happens and I'm stuck at the Camp, I want someone to take care of you and the baby. I'm not sure she could handle that," Vilém said. "Oh, Mama! Speaking of which, I promised Ilona and Ms. Doubek I'd bring the album!"

"You remembered!" squealed Jana happily while Lida retrieved a small leather-bound book full of pictures.

"There! Everyone should be there! We haven't gone through them since Papa passed," Lida sighed. Vilém vowed to take good care of the old memories, kissed his mother and fiancée goodbye, and hugged his father.

"You look like you're about to go into battle, my boy," Tomas whispered into his son's ear.

"I guess I kinda am, Pap."

"Chin up. You're a tough boy. Whoever's pissing you off, give 'em Hell."

"So, Rehor, have you come up with a way to get rid of our little pest?"

"I think I have, though it may require some danger..." Vilém replied as he marched into his boss' office. Ms. Doubek was rifling through a small stack of pictures. She saw that he was holding a leather-bound book and held out her hand, offering him a smile. Vilém grinned and gave her the album. Ever since he had made her laugh in

Barrack Two, Ms. Doubek had become much nicer. Not sweet as sugar, and she still didn't abide by nonsense, but she showed off her smile once a day now, usually reserving it for him.

"Thank you! You already showed Ilona?" Alica said, rifling through Vilém's family photos. He nodded.

"Uh huh, and digitized them, if you need digital copies..."

"I'll handle that, and I can restore them a bit," Ms. Doubek said, meeting the frozen eyes of little Fabian Svoboda and letting a lovely smile grace her wrinkled face. "These will do well! I think it's about time we gave the survivors some love."

"So the Heydrich Exhibit's going down and the Survivor Exhibit will be in Barrack Four, right? I wanted to take my mom, and if possible Ilona..."

"Oh, of course! I may need some quotes and statements from Ilona, and since your grandfather's passed maybe your mother could tell us a few things. Or you could!"

"I could, but my grandpa wasn't at the Camp...we always kind of assumed he was. But he never really talked much about the war, so we only really knew that Sam was on Klammer's Train. But, well, Klammer showed me his memories and Grandpa and Great-Grandma Rebecca weren't here. My great-uncle was here, though. I could tell you about him or I could call his kids."

"That would work...hm...I'm just wondering about aesthetics right now..." Ms. Doubek sighed and glanced out the window, peering at the few solemn visitors that remained at the Camp. "You think an exhibit like this will be...appropriate? I know the guests will like it, they hate leaving the Camp completely depressed, but it seems like..."

"The Holocaust isn't just about the dead, Alica," Vilém said, leaning over the desk and gesturing towards the image of Sam Svoboda. "If it was, we wouldn't have to talk about it so much. We should show how people lived after it...the fact that they lived on after it, that's a kick to the balls for Hitler and Heydrich, and Gerber too."

"Gerber! Yes, I almost forgot!" Alica cried, shuffling the papers and pictures into a neat stack and then twirling her finger impatiently at Vilém. "Come on, come on, tell me what you found! I want to get rid of this bastard as quickly as possible. I doubt he'll appreciate the Survivor Exhibit, and I don't want him making trouble."

"I found some info about his personal life, enough that I think if I can get to him, talk to him on my terms, then maybe I could get him out."

"That would require knowing where he stays. He goes to every barrack and never seems to linger for very long."

"True. But everyone else stayed where they had a reason to stay, and he has most reason to stay at..."

"His old house," sighed Alica, plopping her papers into an accordion folder and biting her bottom lip. "Barrack One."

"It's the only place we haven't checked."

"And it's the only place you can't get into," Alica said, trotting towards the window and parting the curtains enough that she could see a distant corner of the camp. An old building stood in the shadows, blocked off by yellow tape and thick wire fencing.

"I was hoping you could..." Vilém started to say, but Alica shook her head.

"Vilém, I don't own the Camp, and that building is supposed to be preserved for historical studies only. We're not supposed to let anyone go in there unless they're sent by the government for restoration. Amateur historians and students have to wait months to get permission to go in, and they have to be supervised to make sure they don't touch anything. If you went in there without the proper papers, I would *have* to fire you. It would be out of my hands...and you would never get permission to go 'conduct research' in there after dark."

"I understand, Ms. Doubek," Vilém sighed.

"I...would rather not fire you, Vilém," Ms. Doubek said, releasing the curtain and facing him with her lips upturned. "You were going to be my employee of the month."

"You're joking!" laughed Vilém.

"Most of my employees just get drunk and lounge around all night, maybe chase some teenagers away. If I'd known you had to deal with all these ghosts, I may have paid you better."

"You could always give me a bonu—"

"No."

"Worth a shot," Vilém snickered. "In all seriousness, I'll take the risk."

"Vilém, you are about to have a child, I don't want to fire you and have you..."

"I won't starve. We'll still have the sweet shop. It'll be hard, but I'll live. This is important. You're right: he won't like the Survivor Exhibit, and I don't want anyone else getting hurt."

He gestured towards his eyes and Ms. Doubek's wrinkled hands curled into shaking fists. She nodded.

"Very well...I'll cover for you as much as I can, but we never had this conversation. If you can manage this without disturbing anything in Barrack One, all's well, but if you can't...I'm sorry."

"It's not your fault, Ms. Doubek," Vilém said, grabbing his family album and hugging it to his chest, trying to draw strength from the images of his ancestors. "This is all Gerber's fault. I'm gonna make sure he knows that."

Sneaking into Barrack One proved relatively easy. Ms. Doubek made sure to "accidentally" leave the key on her desk, and once he "stole" it, getting into the barrack was simply a matter of climbing over the tape, snipping some wire, and reaching the too-familiar front door.

He squeezed his family album. He had brought it with him just in case he needed ammunition against the Kommandant, to show him how thoroughly he had failed. Gripping the leather book like a child might a teddy bear, he looked up at the weathered building. The paint had chipped and fallen away, revealing the "Barrack One" plaque that Hans Gerber had been determined to hide.

Vilém took out the key and jabbed it into the rusted doorknob. The ancient door shrieked as he opened it, revealing a gloomy interior. The electricity must have been cut long ago, when the Communist government of Czechoslovakia had restricted access to the Kommandant's house. Why such a decision had been made was a mystery. Perhaps they hadn't wanted Fascists to turn the house into a memorial. Perhaps the Reds had not liked the notion of people entering the building and seeing little pieces of humanity. Perhaps they didn't like to be reminded of how similar they were to the Fascists they had fought.

Vilém tarried at the threshold of the forbidden property. The modern Czech government didn't want grubby gross men getting their grubby gross hands all over the little piece of frozen time. Touching anything was not only governmental grounds for dismissal, it was illegal. And though Vilém was willing to do almost anything to get rid of the Nazi, he didn't want to be a criminal. Ms. Doubek was right. He had a child to worry about.

But before he could let fear conquer his heart, he felt a warm burst of defiance. Where it came from he wasn't sure, but it felt like a gentle push, like someone had just grabbed his hand and promised him that he wasn't alone.

He stepped in, and although he could sense that the Kommandant's former residence was awash in a cold aura, whatever force stood by him kept it at bay, bathing him in comforting warmth and allowing him to journey through the house without shivering.

He peeked out a nearby window and saw that Iveta's old doghouse was gone, probably thrown out when she had been moved to Barrack Four. He wouldn't find the Kommandant there. He decided to check Gerber's old office. It was so identical to how it had looked a hundred years ago that it felt like stepping into a memory. The desk was the same, the Nazi books lining the shelves were all there, there was even a scowling bust of Hitler on the mantle. He touched everything he could, even poking the Hitler bust's moustache, but he found nothing.

He checked Raya's old developing room next, which was bare except for a few empty chemical tubs and the broken bits of the Kommandant's camera, which rested in a display case in the corner. Vilém scowled at the shattered camera lens, looking at his reflection in the foggy glass. He touched the display case, then lifted it and touched the camera. Nothing.

One more possibility. Vilém left the developing room and stumbled into the nursery. Most of Martin's toys had been preserved, though they sat behind glass now instead of laying hither and thither.

Vilém felt something right away, a pull towards one particular toy: a ragged little stuffed cat with onyx button eyes. It rested separate from the others, lying outside of the glass on the little twin bed right beside the pillow. Vilém squinted at it. It looked familiar...yes, he remembered it from Klammer and Doctor Doubek's respective memories. Martin had been holding it on his not-birthday, the day before the Freedom Train left the Camp.

Vilém, not wanting to test the strength of the bed, sat on the ground and gingerly picked up the toy. He cradled it in his arms and closed his eyes.

"Heydrich told me about Isaac," he called out, and he felt a burst of surprise come from the malicious spirit.

Asshole.

"Enough with the menacing boom in your voice, Gerber, I've already figured you out. Your dad sacrificed his life for a Jew, and you blame all of them for that. It's simple."

Nothing is ever that simple, Czech.

"Would you care to enlighten me, then?"

Ha! Cute. Are you here to save my soul, Czech?

"Not really. I'm curious."

Ask that cat about curiosity.

"If I managed to squeeze info out of Heydrich, I'll squeeze it out of you, Gerber."

Heydrich was always weak. Sentimental.

Vilém snorted. "The Blonde Beast? Sentimental?"

Oh, he always droned on and on with excuses and justifications. He was always content to write orders for Jew deaths, but he never wanted to see it up close. Always got so squeamish when I showed him pictures. He always avoided the prisoners and the barracks when he came to the Camp. He was a glorified paper-pusher. He didn't have a warrior's heart.

"And you did? You liked making the Jews suffer?"

Is it so strange to enjoy an enemy's pain? Would you not indulge in my suffering, Czech?

"Yeah, but you're actually evil. You just decided that all Jews are evil because...well, because."

Because of many factors. Look at the world...look how they've corrupted your culture, look how they've...

"I didn't come for a Hitlerian sermon, Gerber, I came for a story. Your story."

Really? Hm...I am curious, how are you able to talk to us?

"I wouldn't know."

Don't lie, Czech! I know you've been working with the Jews, and I know you made it your mission to release them, to make them move on...

"I get it. You're upset I helped them. You wanted me to let them stay here forever. Miserable. With you."

They deserved it.

"You deserve it, they didn't. But I've been through the Camp a hundred times looking for you. I know you're the last one here. You lost. You're alone."

Yes...I suppose I am. There were a few seconds of bitter silence between the Czech and the Nazi as the Kommandant seemed to mull over this fact for the first time in weeks. Vilém felt the slightest twinge of sadness echo from the depths of the wicked soul.

I'd rather not be alone here, and there is one thing I need to know. And you...you may be able to help me.

"I don't wanna help you, I wanna get rid of you," Vilém hissed.

Same difference. I'm not leaving until I get what I want.

"Fine, but let's make this quick. I don't want to see too much from your point of view."

Pity, that, but I suppose you Czechs are ever so intellectually...uncurious.

"Said the man whose ideology is known for burning

books," Vilém countered, earning a small chuckle from the Nazi spirit.

Well...fair point. If you help me, I'll refrain from attacking you again. How's that for a deal, Czech?

"And you'll leave?"

Hm...well, I'm not sure. I don't know what comes after this.

"Scared of Hell, Nazi?" Vilém teased, and the Kommandant scoffed.

If there is a God, and He is all merciful, then whatever Hell He designed is preferable to staying here and hearing ignorant lamentations and Jew crocodile tears from dawn till dusk. So...no, I'm not afraid of Hell.

"Good, I'm sure you have a reserved seat. Let's get you down there as fast as possible."

Don't rush me, Czech. I'm being rather generous, allowing a mutt like you to see my memories. They're precious, and you don't deserve them. But...you must look. Seeing may make all the difference. Now...I suppose we'll start with Martin. Senior, that is.

Vilém almost yelped as he was shoved into Gerber's memory: the Kommandant, unlike every other ghost, was forceful. It felt as though the Nazi had grabbed him by the throat and thrown him into a deep pit. When Vilém opened his eyes and found himself in the past, he was so dizzy that it took him a second to get his bearings and actually see through Gerber's eyes.

He settled into the body, which was that of a very young Hans Gerber. The picture of innocence so far: Vilém felt nothing but childish awe flowing through the little boy's body as he peered out his window and gawked at a marching troop. Vilém saw little spikes on the helmets of the German soldiers and realized they were off to WWI, off to die in the trenches.

Comfortable? The Kommandant's snide intrusion reminded Vilém of who he was occupying.

"For now. You're not evil yet."

Children are foolish, but adults were as well back then. They didn't realize how the Jews would rob them...they marched alongside the German-speaking Jews who infiltrated their ranks, genuinely believing they wouldn't stab them in the back...

"Pipe down, I'm not going to learn anything if you recite a passage from *Mein Kampf* every time a new memory starts."

So uncurious...fine. Well, you know what happened to my father, but at the time...well, he was invincible to me. I was only five. I didn't think anything could hurt him...

Vilém felt the child's eyes focus on one soldier in particular, a dead-ringer for the Aryan superman who marched behind one company, holding an Imperial German flag. Little Hans Gerber squealed and ran out of his nursery.

"Hansie, don't...!" A woman wearing a worried expression, presumably little Hans' mother, leapt from her seat at a grand piano and tried to stop her son. Vilém only got a brief look at the interior of Hans' house, but judging from the polished piano that lay in the finery-clad living room, the Gerbers were well off.

"Papie, Papie!" Hans squeaked as he burst out of the house and barreled towards the parade. A small crowd of onlookers stood in his way, waving flags and blowing kisses to their departing loved ones. Little Hans didn't let them stop him, however. He crawled towards the soldiers, weaving through the civilians' legs until he emerged on the other side of the throng. He found his father amongst the marching men and ran towards him, causing the onlookers to laugh and cry, "Aww!"

"Hansie, you little sneak!" Martin Senior laughed, scooping his child into one arm, making sure to hold the flag up high and proud. Hans wrapped his arms around his father's neck, giggling as the tassels on the flag tickled his nose.

"Mama wants to go to Paris, Papie!" Hans announced. "Can we go too? Are you sure we can't go? Papie, pleeeease?"

"Hans, by the time I come back, Germany will *own* Paris!" laughed Martin Senior. "We can go there whenever we want and we'll take lots of pictures!"

Ah...yes. When I was little, I loved picture books. Papa used to make them for me. We had a camera—something of a luxury back then! He would go places and take pictures and Mother would sew them into a little book for me.

"Hm...you really loved your father," Vilém observed.

He was a good man. He was never distant...always kind, loyal, and loving in a way many fathers were not back then. Any other father would have beaten me senseless for interrupting a parade. Not him.

"Apple fell far from the tree, then," grumbled Vilém. Little Hans kissed his father's cheek and Martin Senior put him down.

"Be good!" Martin Senior commanded. "Help your mother, don't be a leech!"

"Yes, sir!" Hans cried, saluting his father. Vilém could feel the child's heart swelling, and he could only hope that his child would feel the same overwhelming sense of adoration whenever they looked up at him.

In the blink of an eye, Martin Senior was gone and Hans, a year older, was in his living room, sitting beside his mother. Frau Gerber was unfolding a letter.

"Lemme see the pictures! Lemme see the pictures!" Hansie begged, reaching for the letter and whining when his mother refused to hand it over right away, insisting on reading it over before she let him see it. Hans threw an absolute tantrum at not getting what he wanted right away.

"Lemme see, lemme see!" he cried, smacking the chair so hard that his little fists ached. Vilém scoffed.

"You were a real spoiled brat," Vilém said. "Guess I can see where the entitlement came from."

That's a bit of a stretch. I admit to being spoiled as a child, but I don't see what that has to do with my eventual political views.

"You didn't get what you wanted when you were a kid, you threw a fit and punched furniture. You didn't get what you wanted as an adult, you threw a fit and killed Jews."

Hm. The Führer didn't have the cushy childhood I did, nor did Heydrich.

"Fine, you're not wrong. It's a factor, not the *only* reason."

I would argue it's not a factor at all, but that's beside the point.

"All right, all right, sweetie," Frau Gerber sighed, picking up her writhing son and plopping him on her lap. He settled as soon as he got what he wanted, grinning as she showed him the message. Martin Senior had formatted the letter carefully, pasting several pictures next to the paragraphs.

"Papa says he's made friends with all the men in his company. Papa's guarding a small border town in the Austro-Hungarian Empire," Frau Gerber explained, gesturing to a picture of a grinning Martin Senior standing in a trench, hugging a gas mask to his chest.

"He says he's made friends with a man named Friedrich, there they are..." A picture of Martin Senior and his grinning comrade sharing a chocolate bar.

"He also says the people in town are very nice and give them flowers all the time!"

She pointed to the last picture: Martin Senior was clutching a bouquet and patting a little boy on the head. The boy had curly ebony hair. His facial structure was familiar.

"That's him?" Vilém asked.

Isaac Goldstein. My age. He was a big fan of the military. Liked to give the soldiers treats and get a little too close to the trenches. But I don't think I can blame him too much for that. In the early days, the war was a fun affair. It was all about honor and glory, but then...things became worse. Pictures became more and more scarce, and one day...

The memory shifted in the blink of an eye. One

moment little Hans was sitting in his mother's lap, staring at his smiling father's image, and the next he was older, hiding under the piano seat. He was lying with his cheek on the ground, hugging a bound book of pictures and staring at the front door. A German soldier was talking to a hysterical Frau Gerber, half-hugging her. Hans' ears were ringing, his heart was beating so loud he only heard little shreds of the soldier's speech.

"Hero...sacrificed...gas attack...village...this boy..."

The soldier gestured to his side, and Hans' eyes widened when he saw a tiny figure peeking out from behind the man's pant leg. A small child with curly dark hair. Isaac Goldstein lifted his eyes from his grime-covered shoes and sheepishly met Hans' gaze.

Well...the Allies attacked, the village got hit by gas while my father was there...he gave his gas mask to Isaac. He died to save Isaac's life.

"And you're bitter about that? Is that it?" Vilém queried.

Not precisely. My father was a hero...he died a hero, died to save this boy's life. Isaac's parents died in the gas attack, and my mother decided to take him in. We had the space, and we...didn't want my father to have died for nothing. I didn't mind the idea at first. It felt...nice to have him there. It was like he was a little piece of my father, like my father lived on through him.

"Isaac, catch!"

A new memory formed. Hans stood in the backyard of his sprawling home, heart racing, blood pumping. He hurled a ball at little Isaac, who had traded his scrappy peasant clothes for fine, soft garments. Isaac was prodding at the grass with a stick, drowning in his own thoughts.

"Isaac!" Hans cried, and the ball struck Isaac's head. The Jewish boy fell to the ground, clutching his skull.

"Oooowwww, Hans!" whined Isaac, rolling onto his back. Hans scurried to his friend's side and stood above him, smirking.

"I warned ya!" Hans giggled. Isaac grunted, grabbing a fistful of grass and yanking it out of the dirt.

"I was *thinking*, you ass!" the Jewish child snapped, tossing the grass at Hans, who squealed and reached down, pulling a mass of dirt, grass, and roots out of the ground.

"Dirty Jew!" Hans laughed, throwing the dirt at Isaac, who barely dodged his friend's assault. Isaac squatted on the damaged lawn, scowling at Hans even as a slight smile forced its way onto his solemn face.

"Don't call me that, that's not funny!" Isaac cried, tugging a chunk of the lawn from the ground and hurling it at Hans.

"You *are* a dirty Jew right now, look at you! You've got dirt on your ass!" Hans replied playfully.

"And you're a dirty goy!" Isaac retorted, ducking behind a tree and yanking a vine off the trunk, trying to use it as a makeshift whip to beat his brother. Hans found his own tree to hide behind, grabbing as much dirt and grass as his little fists could hold.

"Whoever gets dirtiest is the loser!" Hans dared. "Loser's gotta clean the winner's room!"

"You're on, but I get the first bath!" Isaac snickered, and Hans blew out an agitated breath.

"Damn it..." Hans muttered. The boys roared like soldiers as they charged at each other, flinging mud and rubbing grass into each other's clothes. By the time the battle was done and Isaac was declared the victor, the lawn was in ruins, both boys were coated in filth, and they were laughing themselves stupid. Right then, it seemed like they really were brothers.

It was good...for some time. When we were both little, we got along. I...cared for Isaac. He was a friend, a brother...it seemed to me that my father had died for a good reason, to let this boy live.

"...But?"

We grew, and he changed.

Hans blinked and the memory shifted. He and Isaac, now clean and pressed, were standing in front of a mirror. Frau Gerber was brushing Hans' hair, smiling down at her son. Vilém noticed that Isaac's satchel was worn down while Hans' looked brand new.

"Be good for your new teacher, Hansie," Frau Gerber cooed at her child.

"Yes, Mama!" Hans chirped.

Frau Gerber stepped behind Isaac and roughly ran her brush through his hair, grunting when his tangled curls offered resistance and giving up right away, handing Isaac the hairbrush.

"You'll have to manage it yourself, Isaac," she said. Isaac nodded slowly, reaching up and wincing as he combed his own hair. Vilém could see tears shining in his eyes.

"You need to try harder this year, Isaac," Frau Gerber commanded, standing over Isaac's shoulder and scowling at the Jewish child's reflection. "Your grades last year were not acceptable."

"Yes, ma'am," sighed Isaac, giving up on his hair and handing the brush back to Hans' mother.

"Wow, your mom definitely *didn't* pick favorites," Vilém muttered sarcastically as Frau Gerber snatched the brush out of Isaac's hand and sent the boys off, kissing Hans tenderly on the cheek and banishing Isaac with a dismissive wave.

Isaac was not her son. She had no obligation towards him. No obligation to treat him as her own. She didn't have to take him in, yet she did out of kindness. He should have appreciated that without demanding more.

"She took him in, she should have treated him the same as you. He didn't choose to lose his family, he didn't choose to be taken in by people who didn't love him."

We did love him!

"Taking someone in and making them feel bad for being alive constantly, treating them like a burden and telling them they should be grateful for scraps...that's not love."

You sound just like him...

"Try having some empathy for once, Gerber!" Vilém snapped, watching as Hans walked two steps ahead of Isaac, occasionally glancing back at the Jewish boy. Isaac was dragging his feet, looking from his worn-down shoes to Hans' brand new boots.

"How would you feel?" Vilém asked. "If you lost your mother and father and everything else and suddenly found yourself in his situation, how would you feel?"

I would show gratitude and understand how trouble-some I was. I'd understand the sacrifice the family had made and I'd never complain.

"I'm sure you'd *love* to be treated as second-class..." muttered Vilém.

At the time, we were second class. Germany's victory was stolen. We were betrayed, we were robbed, and our currency became worthless. We were the world's second-class citizens...

"Hey, Jew!"

Hans heard a grunt and Vilém felt the boy's heart cartwheel against his chest. Surprise, however, didn't strike him. Instead, it was a familiar sense of dread, the sort of feeling that Vilém had experienced whenever he had gone to class on test day knowing he had not studied, expecting to fail, expecting to be humiliated.

Hans turned just in time to see a small pack of hooligans surround Isaac. One of them, a dark-haired boy who might have passed for a stereotypical Jew himself, grabbed Isaac's satchel and dumped the heavy books on the Jewish boy's head.

Vilém felt Hans' cheeks flush. The young German scrambled inside the nearest shop, pressing his face against the glass, watching from the window as the boys tormented Isaac.

"Here, Jew, here! Have some money!" the pack leader sneered, and he and his comrades pulled little stacks of paper out of their bags and tossed it at the Jew. Vilém almost wanted to laugh when he realized they were attacking their victim with piles of Reichsmarks, rendered worthless by the post-war hyperinflation. The sight might have been funny if it weren't at the expense of the already-downtrodden boy. Isaac curled into a little ball, trying to cover his face. The boys laughed and the leader grabbed Isaac by his satchel, forcing him to his feet.

The big guy there is Derek. Lived on our block once, but the Depression ruined his family. We continued to have a somewhat cordial relationship, but he didn't like Isaac at all.

"Obviously," Vilém growled as Derek and his goons started shoving the worthless bills into Isaac's mouth, nearly choking the child with Marks.

Isaac was a Jew by blood alone. At our home, he never attempted to celebrate Jewish holidays. He attended church with us, celebrated Christmas with us...but he still insisted on calling himself a Jew. I wonder why.

"Pride?" Vilém suggested, and the Nazi spirit sneered.

Jews have nothing to be proud of.

Little Hans watched as Isaac was beaten and humiliated, and yet neither pity nor guilt entered the child's soul. He felt embarrassed, he felt irate, he tapped his foot as though this entire affair was a waste of *his* time. He never looked at his so-called brother's turmoil with empathy, and the impulse to go out and help was nonexistent.

"Wow..." Vilém whispered. "You really were a little bastard."

What was I supposed to do? Defend him?

"Uhm...yes."

I was already unpopular because of him. I suffered many indignities on his behalf because we were kind enough to take him in after my father gave his life for him. The least he could have done was handle some bullying with grace. I had no obligations towards him.

"With this kind of environment, I wonder what might have fucked him up," Vilém scoffed. "I bet I'd be mentally healthy if my so-called brother was refusing to help me and constantly guilting me for killing his father."

He DID kill my father! And all we ever asked of him was that he make something of himself, make it so that my father didn't die for nothing! But no! No, he had to be self-ish! He had to act like a child!

"He *was* a child!" Vilém cried as the bullies grew tired of their quarry and dropped Isaac on the ground, giving him a few final kicks for good measure. They giggled and scattered, Derek pausing outside the window of the shop. He tapped on the glass in front of Hans' face, offering the German boy a small smile and gesturing towards Isaac.

"Hey, Gerber," Derek sneered. "You can have your Jew back."

"...Thanks..." Hans sighed, waving farewell as Derek darted off. Once he was sure that the bullies were gone, Hans exited the shop and slowly approached Isaac, who was sitting in a pile of Marks, crying.

"C'mon, Isaac," Hans said. "We're gonna be late for school."

"You go."

"Mama said..."

"I don't care what *your* mother said!" Isaac hissed, finally lifting his eyes. Hans jumped back as though he had just touched a hot stove, the furious fire in Isaac's irises shocking and upsetting him far more than Derek's attack had.

Anger jabbed at Hans' heart, and Vilém could hardly believe it. It seemed strange to him, that anyone could be so blind to how terrible they were, but Hans right then felt moral outrage, as though Isaac had beaten *him* up.

"Fine!" Hans hissed. "I don't wanna be seen with you anyway!"

Vilém felt a tiny, weak strike at Hans' soul. The part of him that loved Isaac, the part that wanted to go to school with him and be his brother, tried to assuage his pride and convince him to take that back. But Hans' ego was stronger. He turned, wiped his eyes...

And the memory shifted. Hans was a teenager now, his face covered with a fencer's mask. An eager, energetic rush filled his veins as he swung his saber at his opponent. With a dodge and a stab, he claimed victory, jabbing his opponent in the chest.

"Fuck!" his opponent cried, ripping off his mask and revealing himself to be Derek. Isaac's bully seemed sour for a moment, but the referee chastised him for being a poor sport and he seemed to remember his honor.

"Sorry, coach," Derek sighed. He reached out and grasped Hans' hand.

"I sometimes forget we're on the same team," Derek chuckled. "Just be sure to do that shit when we go up against Kiel."

"Will do!" Hans laughed, following his brother's bully back to the benches. They sat beside one another, chatting casually, and Vilém huffed.

"Reeeeal nice," he said. "Getting all buddy-buddy with someone who hates your brother."

Should I have cut contact? Refused Derek's friend-ship because of his views? Should I have lingered in the shadows with Isaac?

"Yes, Gerber! Yes, that is what you should have done! I can't believe you can't see this!" snapped Vilém. "You are *such* a shitty person and you don't even realize it! Good people don't betray people they claim to love! Good people stand by the victim, not the bully!"

Derek acted as a child would when he was younger. He knew about the wider Jewish Problem and behaved immaturely, but he mellowed over time.

"Ooooh, so he became a *polite* anti-Semite, I get it," sneered Vilém. "That makes it *so* much better!"

You're rather caustic.

"*You're* rather toxic," Vilém retorted as Derek left Hans on the benches, running outside for only a few seconds before darting back in with a vicious smirk on his face. He sat down beside Hans again and leaned close to his ear.

"Hey, Hans, your Jew is by the outhouse again."

"Shit, how big's the bottle?" Hans asked, and Derek held his hands a fair distance apart.

"Cover for me, please," Hans begged, and Derek nodded, still wearing an insufferable expression of giddiness even as his so-called "friend" ran from the gym with distress decorating his face.

Hans exited the building and glanced at the outhouses, spotting a figure sitting beside them. With an agitated huff, Hans approached Isaac, who was now sporting a patchy beard. Isaac's hair was long and unruly, as though he had completely given up trying to comb it, and he had almost finished off a tall bottle of what, based on the smell, Vilém assumed was either whisky or some kind of moonshine.

Around the time we turned sixteen, he started drinking. He stopped coming to school except to drink and loiter around the building...

"Can't imagine what might have driven him to drink..." Vilém hissed as young Hans knelt before his not-brother and reached out, trying to grab the bottle. Isaac, so drunk that he could barely move, moaned in agitation and hugged the bottle to his chest.

"Isaac, enough of this!" snapped Hans. "Mother said you're not allowed to drink anymore!"

"Well, she's not my mother, is she?" sneered Isaac, taking a defiant swig from the bottle. Hans used the opportunity to steal the alcohol from the Jewish teen, yanking it out of his weak grasp and emptying the bottle's contents into the grass.

"Jackass!" snarled Isaac, attempting to stand but immediately collapsing. Hans rolled his eyes and threw the empty bottle at Isaac's feet.

"This is pure foolishness, Isaac!" Hans sighed. "You're supposed to be in class!"

"Who cares about class? The fucking teacher'll fail me anyway," grumbled Isaac. "Even if they don't, I won't be able to focus. Your fencing friend will just steal my fucking notebook again and again..." Isaac sat up, swaying slightly as he scowled at Hans. "How're you enjoying fencing club?"

"Isaac, please, not this again..."

"Bet it's fun. You don't have to deal with any dirty Jews in there since they don't let us join. You don't have to be embarrassed about me existing..."

"I wouldn't be embarrassed by you if you would just shape up, Isaac!" shouted Hans, squatting down to Isaac's level and jabbing his not-brother in the chest with his index finger. "We ask very little of you, only that you try to make something of yourself!"

"I *am* making something of myself, Hansie," hissed Isaac, grabbing a handful of dirt and shoving it in Hans' face. Hans sputtered and recoiled, anger filling his every atom.

"You dirty Jew!" snapped Hans, and gone was the affectionate teasing that had been present when he had uttered those words as a child. His voice was filled with nothing but anger.

He lunged at Isaac, but the Jew grabbed the empty bottle and swung it, striking Hans on the shoulder. The glass shattered and the teenager tumbled to the ground. He lay there, stunned, breathing in brief spurts, and Isaac lay beside him, too drunk to run.

Hans stared up at the bright blue sky, fury and sorrow flooding him. He grabbed his throbbing head.

"I hate you..." Hans sniffled, failing to hold in a sob.

"Yeah...I know..." sighed Isaac.

"I wish Papa was alive and you were dead," Hans hiccupped, covering his face with his arm, shame attacking his soul. He must have looked terrible right then. Like a dirty weakling. Like a dirty Jew.

"I know..." Isaac whispered.

Hans wiped his tears away. "Please go to class, Isaac, please..."

"I didn't ask for this shit, Hansie," Isaac muttered, ignoring Hans' plea. "I didn't ask to be your Jew. I didn't wanna be with your family."

"'Your'?" Vilém repeated.

He was always a guest, Czech.

"You made him feel like a pest," Vilém accused.

Young Hans rolled over, facing Isaac. When he saw that the young Jew had pearls of salty water rolling down his cheeks, he finally allowed pity to fill his heart.

"If I quit fencing...will you go to class?" Hans asked. Isaac's lips quirked up into an almost-smile.

"Promise?" he asked, his voice bitter, as though he had been offered this very deal one too many times.

"Yeah...and you can borrow my notes for class...if you need them," Hans vowed. "Please, Isaac, don't make all of this pointless."

Isaac stared up at the sky for a few moments before turning to face Hans. He nodded once, wiping his face with his mud-covered hand and leaving a grimy streak on his cheek. Hans giggled.

"You...you *are* a dirty Jew!" he hiccupped, grabbing a handful of grass and shoving it in Isaac's face. The Jew snickered and rolled away.

"Ouch!" Isaac cried, lifting his palm, which had a shard of glass stuck in it. Hans started to stand, laughing.

"Serves you right, you drunk—OW!" Before he could truly tease Isaac for his injury, Hans cut himself on a piece of the broken bottle. The two teens looked at one another, glanced at each other's wounds, and both cackled.

"Hey, here!" Hans said, opening his injured palm towards Isaac. "Get some German blood in ya', maybe you'll do better in class."

"Get some Jew blood in you, maybe you'll be less of an ass," Isaac countered, and both boys shook hands, letting their blood mix.

Didn't I tell you? I gave him a chance...but he kept squandering it.

"Well...did you go back to fencing class?" Vilém queried.

Well, eventually, but...

"And did you keep speaking to Derek?"

I...

"And did your mother ever treat him like an equal?"

Well, she...

"Yes or no?"

No, but...

"Kinda funny. Heydrich said you used to describe Isaac as a nightmare. Really, though...you sound like the worst. I have four little sisters, and I can't *imagine* doing this kind of shit to them and then pretending to be the victim."

Your sisters are your blood!

"You made a blood pact with Isaac. You adopted him. You should have treated him like a brother, not a project."

Ha! Well, if Isaac was a project, he was a failed one. He dropped out of school at a young age...kept drink-

ing...never managed to keep a job no matter what we did. Granted, at the time it was difficult for anyone to get a job.

"I'm very sorry, son, but we really don't need a photographer right now." A new memory formed. Hans, heart falling, stumbled out of a building, led by an old, kind-eyed man.

"If I get any openings, I'll call you...there are other newspapers in town, though! Talent like yours, you'll find something!" the old man declared.

"Thank you, sir..." muttered Hans, anger boiling in his blood. He hurried away from the editor as quickly as he could, ducking into an alleyway and slamming his fist against a wall. The petulant act made his hand ache, but he didn't care. He just wanted to punch the wall, punch something, punch someone...

"Hey! Hey, Hans!"

Hans turned to the mouth of the alley, shoving his fist into his pocket and repressing a pained expression. Vilém wasn't surprised to see Derek standing there, and he was even less surprised that the bully was sporting a swastika armband and a black SS uniform. Hans, however, evidently was surprised. He raised an eyebrow at Isaac's old foe.

"Derek, what's with the getup?" he asked. Derek glanced down at his SS uniform and grinned like a missionary that had just been asked a question about Jesus.

"SS! You haven't heard of it?"

"I've heard of the SA," Hans said, gesturing towards a candy shop across the street. "They got into a fight with some Reds a few days ago and nearly killed the shopkeeper."

"The SA are a bunch of degenerate brutes," Derek said with a nod. "Hitler shouldn't bother with them, and he won't bother with them for much longer."

"Hitler? Oh, Derek, you know his party's illegal right now..."

"But it won't be for much longer, it's been banned and unbanned five times!" Derek argued. "Besides, Hitler's blossoming into a real politician, he's not just a street-brawling ruffian anymore. He has a proper plan, and the SS is going to be his elite unit to combat the Reds and restore Germany's dignity!"

"You know I'm not very political, Derek," sighed Hans. "Besides, I've heard what they have to say about Jews and...well...Isaac."

"Isaac, yes, but isn't Isaac sort of the...posterboy of those views?" Derek said. "Speaking of Isaac, though, he got caught again."

"Fuck! Again!" Hans snarled, barely repressing the urge to punch the bricks again. Derek nodded.

"Yep, he's lying in the alley behind the bar. Again. You may wanna grab him before the Brownshirts do. And listen...if you joined the SS, it would give you *and* Isaac security. You could protect him. He gets into so much trouble and...if the Führer wins, Jews like him will be dealt with harshly. I don't like him, but I know that would upset you..."

"Yes..." whispered Hans, pulling his throbbing hand from his pocket and wiggling his fingers, perhaps imagining what they would look like covered by a black glove.

"And we have a lot of extra programs! We're forming our own newspaper, so you could probably get a photography job! And there's even a fencing club! We take physical fitness very seriously!"

"All right, all right, I'll think about it!" laughed Hans. "Quit missionizing, I've gotta go get Isaac!"

"Fine, but let's get a beer later and talk about it more!" Derek suggested.

"If the barkeeper doesn't ban my whole family," grumbled Hans. He bade Derek farewell and rushed out of the alley, hurrying down the block. He found a small hole-in-the-wall bar situated beside an alley that looked ripe for mugging. Its dangerous appearance wasn't helped by the fact that when he looked, he saw a figure sitting beside the garbage cans. He scoffed and marched into the foreboding alley, grabbing a besodden Isaac by the arm and dragging him to his feet.

"Get up, asshole!" Hans commanded. "I've told you not to steal anymore! You're lucky he didn't kill you this time."

"How else am I supposed to get a damn drink around here?" slurred Isaac. Hans slung the Jew's arm over his shoulders.

"You shouldn't! You're not supposed to be drinking at all, we talked about this!" huffed Hans. "You never listen!"

"Frau Gerber gives *you* money every week and ya' don't have a job either."

"That's because *I* don't spend *my* money on booze, Isaac."

"I didn't get an allowance...even before I drank..." muttered Isaac. Hans rolled his eyes.

"Would it kill you to put the past behind you?" he snapped, and Isaac turned his cloudy eyes towards the German, hatred burning in his dark irises.

"Would it kill *you*?" he countered, and the memory faded.

His drunkenness...his inability to find work or be useful to society...all of that I could have dealt with. But the final straw came when my mother died. I waited and waited, but...he never showed up to the funeral.

"ISAAC!"

With a brutal kick to the front door of his home, Hans introduced a new memory. The Gerber household was a shadow of its former esteem: the furnishings must have been sold off, the fineries were gone. The home was bare save for the pictures decorating the walls and the piano that still sat in the foyer, which Hans evidently hadn't had the heart to sell.

Isaac was sitting at the piano, leafing through an old bound book of pictures with one hand while the other grasped a bottle. He looked up as Hans entered, smiling joylessly as he held up the book of pictures.

"This is cute..." he said. "Wish my papa had a camera when I was little. I don't even have any pictures 'a him."

"Put! That! Down!" Hans snarled, not giving Isaac time to comply as he marched up to the Jewish man and snatched the picture book from his hands. Hans examined it to make sure it wasn't damaged. Once he confirmed it was pristine, he set it aside and towered over his not-brother.

"You weren't there!" Hans growled, gesturing to the suit he wore. "You weren't there, after everything! After she took you in, protected you...you would be in an orphanage if it weren't for her kindness! You would be a dirty street urchin...and you couldn't even show up to her funeral and say goodbye!"

Hans blinked to keep the tears gathering at the corners of his eyes from escaping. Isaac started idly tapping at the piano keys, creating a sloppy little tune.

"As though she would have cared..." he muttered.

"She would have, Isaac! She would have cared that you sat on your ass and drank during her funeral..."

"Oh, I'm sure! And I'm sure if I'd gone, she would have said I look like a slob! I'm sure I would have gotten a nice suit like yours...oh, but maybe you could'a spared a suit. Maybe...if you'd worn *this* instead."

Isaac tossed the bottle aside, reached under the piano bench, and pulled out a wrinkled black tunic that hung on a hook, a tunic that boasted a swastika armband.

Vilém felt Hans' heart stop as he looked down at his own SS uniform, but embarrassment swiftly morphed into outrage. "You went through my closet!"

"Yeah, I looked through your closet because I was looking for a spare *suit!*" Isaac threw the uniform at Hans, who caught it clumsily. "Because I was gonna go to *your* mom's funeral. But *your mom* never bought *me* nice clothes, so I was scavenging like the dirty little Jew urchin I am. And you..."

Isaac scowled at the swastika. "You despise me

anyway, so why bother going? Why bother with anything?"

"I don't...despise you, you don't understand..." Hans muttered.

"I understand perfectly!" Isaac snarled. "You didn't save me, you stole me! You stole me from my people, you trained me to hate myself, and you succeeded! Are you proud, Hansie? Are you proud of yourself?"

"I...yes, you know what, yes I am!" Hans hissed, grabbing the jacket off the hook and throwing the black SS garment on. He pointed to the swastika and announced. "I'm proud of my race, and I'm proud that my family was generous even to a dirty Jew like you! Even after everything *your* people have done to ours, even after everything *you've* done to me! And I'm proud to be a productive human rather than a waste of not just one, but *two* lives!"

"Proud, ha!" sneered Isaac. "Proud of being born wealthy? Proud of losing a war?"

"We didn't lose anything..."

"Proud of being the laughingstock of Europe?"

"Enough..."

"Oh, I'm sorry! I forgot, you're a Nazi now! Sorry, let me rephrase that...are you proud that you, the superior race...you apparently got trampled by a bunch of dirty Jews?"

"You're going too far!"

"Are you proud of being a loser, Hansie?"

"You need to be quiet..."

"Are you proud of being a Nazi, Hansie?"

"You. Need. To. Be..."

"I bet your dad would be *really* proud of you..."

Vilém had never in his life felt as angry as Hans felt right then. It was as though Isaac had lit a match and set him aflame. Hans, half donning the Nazi uniform, decked Isaac in the face, sending the Jew falling to the floor.

"You be quiet, you lousy Jew!" Hans screeched, leaping on top of Isaac and punching him, punching him over and over and over. "Don't you dare mention my father, you fucking Jew! It's your fault he's dead! It's all your fault!"

Isaac made no attempt to fight back. He lay there, hands at his sides, laughing. He laughed and laughed even as Hans knocked his teeth out, even as Hans broke his nose and covered his cheeks with bruises. Vilém felt a spike of adrenaline shoot through Hans' body with every punch he landed on Isaac, and the Czech guard felt sick. He had, on occasion, harbored animosity towards his sisters, but the feeling of doing this to someone, to someone that a small part of Hans still loved...and to enjoy it this much...

"Enough, enough!" Vilém yelped, and acting as though he had heard the command, young Hans finally ceased his attack. He looked down at Isaac, who was barely breathing. The young Jew could only take short, halting gasps. Vilém was surprised he could even do that. Isaac looked like he'd been hit by a car.

"Isaac...?" Hans muttered. Isaac made no sound to indicate he heard anything, and Vilém was befuddled when worry and guilt started clawing at the young Nazi's soul.

"Isaac! Isaac, you idiot, get up! Get up, you stupid fucking Jew! This is your fault!" Hans insisted, his voice becoming high pitched with panic. Isaac didn't move. Hans reached under Isaac's head, trying to lift him up and carry him to the couch, but he felt a splash of warm liquid as soon as he touched the back of Isaac's head. He pulled his hand out from under the Jew's skull and trembled. His hand was crimson.

"Fuck!" snarled Hans, laying Isaac's head down and rushing up the stairs. He grabbed a small first-aid kit out of a drawer in his room and ran to the phone, dialing the operator and ordering him to call the hospital for him.

"Have them send someone over, fast! My brother is injured!" he begged, hanging up before the operator could say a word and bolting back down to Isaac.

But when he ran into the foyer, all he found was the empty bottle of booze, the trousers of his SS uniform, and a puddle of blood staining the carpet. Isaac was gone, gone without a word.

"Isaac?" cried Hans. The German ran out the semi-ajar front door and looked down the street, in the garden, everywhere he could. He must have figured that the injured Isaac couldn't have gotten far, but search as he might, he couldn't find the Jew.

I never saw him again after that day, and believe me, I tried to find him. For as much as we argued, I didn't want him to die in the streets.

"Yeah, you didn't want your father 'wasting' his sacrifice," scoffed Vilém.

Precisely.

"Maybe this wouldn't have happened if you had

treated him well for his sake instead of tolerating him for your father. Besides, you couldn't have tried *that* hard to find him. You were friends with Heydrich! Heydrich had a file on every Jew in the Reich."

Every Jew except Isaac, apparently. You think I put up with Heydrich because I liked him? Nobody liked Heydrich, and frankly Heydrich didn't like anyone. But time kept marching on, the SS grew in power, I rose through the ranks and learned more and more about the Jews and their...

"What did we say about quoting *Mein Kampf?*"

Uncurious as ever...fine. Point is, I learned how to live in the New Germany, and in the New Germany becoming friends with Heydrich was a benefit. While Heydrich was hardly a social butterfly, he enjoyed sport, especially fencing, and anyone who indulged him earned his respect, if not his affection. And if you earned that, you could get favors...that is, if you were willing to look bad. Heydrich hated to lose.

A new memory started, and Vilém felt Hans' pride screech in agony as the Nazi purposely performed a clumsy swing, leaving himself wide open. Judging by the sweat Vilém could feel on Hans' brow, he had been fencing with the Blonde Beast for some time. Long enough to satisfy the Hangman's thirst for battle, but not long enough to wound Heydrich's fragile ego.

Heydrich easily won the match, tearing off his mask as soon as he landed the final blow and grinning with all the satisfaction of a cat that had just dumped a dead mouse at his master's feet.

"Still undefeated, Gerber!" he sneered, and while

Vilém never thought he would empathize with Hans Gerber, a knife of hatred stabbed him and Hans in unison. Gerber hesitated to take his mask off, perhaps afraid that he wouldn't be able to hide the disdain on his face.

"Good game, Herr Heydrich!" Gerber declared.

"You're one of my best sparring mates!" said Heydrich. "Too bad we won't be attending the Olympics anytime soon. If you and I could be on the team, we'd wipe the floor with the whole world."

"We'll have to kick their asses on the battlefield instead," Hans joked, and Heydrich's lip curled as though he would have liked to chuckle at that, but simply didn't possess enough humanity to allow himself to be seen laughing.

"Of course," the Blonde Beast said, grabbing a towel and wiping his neck. "Did I tell you the good news?"

Vilém felt Hans' heart skip. "Good news, Rein—err, General Heydrich?"

"You're being moved to a new department, directly under my authority. The war is going well, but the Führer wants to focus more on the internal war. The war against the undesirables in our midst. The Jews, the Communists...the traitors."

"Sir...?"

"That wasn't an accusation, Gerber. Trust me...I have my file on you, and while your association with Jews may be...*concerning*...you've been honest with me. And I understand. Everyone has their *Edeljude*. Even Hitler."

"*Edeljude?*" Vilém repeated.

Honorable Jew. Even a vile race is bound to produce a good apple every once in a while. None of us were simple enough to believe that no good Jews existed, it was simply a matter of scale.

"Ha!" laughed Hans. "Well, sir, Isaac Goldstein isn't precisely an honorable Jew. I merely would prefer it if he could have...a higher purpose, whatever higher purpose he may achieve within the Reich."

"A Jew with a higher purpose, hm...how funny..." Heydrich muttered. He winced as though someone had just stepped on his foot and scowled at the ceiling.

"Herr Heydrich?" muttered Hans.

"I'm fine, just a spasm," Heydrich blurted. "As I was saying: I understand your desire to retrieve the Jew Goldstein. Of course, in order to find him, much less be allowed to keep him, you must prove yourself worthy of my time and energy. Put simply: I will find your Jew, but you have to help me plug a leak."

"Leak, sir?"

"Our sources have uncovered a smuggling operation coming out of your hometown, and the contraband is Jews. German Jews are being taken from Gestapo custody, given false papers, and smuggled to Switzerland. And from there? Who knows what sort of damage they could do...who knows what *rumors* they could spread."

"Right...*rumors*," said Hans with a small, grim smirk.

"This is unacceptable, and more so, it means we have a mole. The operation is too advanced to succeed without internal help," Heydrich said.

"SS help?"

"Precisely. Honestly, if I had been forced to dig up your relationship with the Jew Goldstein myself, you would have ended up being my prime suspect. But since you were honest, I believe you have nothing to do with it."

"I'm not fond of Jews, Herr Heydrich."

"No, but one doesn't need to be fond of them in order to be sympathetic. You may not be fond of rats, but if you see one squirming in a trap...well, sadly the German people are often too humane and virtuous for their own good."

"So...you want me to find the mole?"

"Correct, Gerber. Find the mole, plug the hole. We want to solve this Jewish Problem quickly, without inter-ruption. If you can manage this, you'll have stopped perhaps hundreds of Jews from escaping, and I will consider your plea on behalf of the Jew Goldstein to be more than justifiable."

Vilém felt what remained of Hans' conscience object to this exchange, but the young Nazi muted it easily and finally removed his mask, a genuine smile lighting up his face.

"Thank you, sir," he said. "I won't disappoint."

And I didn't...

"Who was the mole?" asked Vilém, and the Nazi ghost snickered.

You'll be as surprised as I was...

A new memory started with a scream as Hans, kneeling before a cellar door, threw the hatch open and shined a flashlight down into the basement. Dozens of eyes shined back. At least fifty "undesirables", most of them children, were huddled together in the tight space. Vilém felt Hans' heart sink, but the Nazi forced it to become hard as iron.

"Gather them!" Hans snapped, and several SS officers obeyed his command, descending into the cellar and pulling out the children by their hair, by their wrists, by their ankles.

"Hans!" A familiar voice, drowning in distress, made Hans turn. Vilém was indeed surprised when he saw the mole. Derek. Isaac's old bully, restrained by two SS officers, watched with horror as the Nazis roughly collected the Jewish children.

"Now, now, Derek, I'm surprised at you!" Hans cried, strutting towards his quarry. The guards holding Derek forced him to kneel before their commander, and though Gerber wore a look of disdain as he towered over Isaac's old bully, Vilém could feel that Hans' chest was writhing.

"From what I remember, you were never a fan of Jewish brats," Hans said. Derek, whose eyes were alight with anger, spat on his old friend's boot.

"They're *children*, Hans!" he snarled, and Hans kicked his ex-friend in the ribs.

"Traitorous bastard," Gerber hissed. "Filthy hypocrite."

"I wanted to send the Jews out of Germany, to send them to Palestine or somewhere else...I *never* signed up to be a murderer!"

"Plans change," Hans said, letting his eyes flit towards one child, a little girl who had decided she would not go without a fight. She scratched and bit the

SS officer who held her, acting like the rabid animal she had been labeled as.

"You've changed, Hans," Derek snapped.

"No...no, I really haven't, but *you* have," Hans insisted. "You've betrayed the Fatherland, you've sheltered enemies of the state..."

"They're just kids, Hans!"

"Jewish whelps will grow into full-grown Jews," Hans said. "They must be dealt with as one deals with newborn rats."

"You don't believe a word of that," sneered Derek. "I get how this works, Hans. You hand over these Jews and Heydrich spares yours. You loved Isaac even though you were always a coward, always too scared to stand up to me..."

Hans smacked Derek across the face, but the former bully laughed even as blood dripped from his split lip.

"Coward!" he cried. "You'll do anything to seem strong, but deep down you're just a stupid little boy still crying about his daddy's death!"

"Enough!" snarled Hans, kicking Derek in the groin. Derek grunted in pain and the two guards restraining him let him fall on his face. Hans slammed his boot on top of the former bully's head.

"Speak of my father again, I dare you..." hissed Hans.

"Your father died for nothing!" Derek sneered. "He died for a pointless war! He died for the enemy! He died for a Jew! And you're going to kill these children to save that one useless Jew!"

Hans put almost all his weight down on Derek's skull, but Derek refused to shut his mouth. "But you're a coward, you always were! You're a coward just like Heydrich! You don't have the guts to put your money where your mouth is!"

It felt like Hans was possessed by the devil. He pulled out his gun, jammed the barrel against Derek's ear. The sound of Derek's laughter was echoing, echoing, the sound of the children screaming, piercing, assaulting his brain. The eyes of the SS officers were watching, judging, ready to report everything. He wanted everyone to stop looking, he wanted everyone to shut up.

"OW!"

One little Jewish girl bit her captor's hand and tried to run to the door. Hans moved on instinct. Everything happened so fast. Raising the gun, hearing Derek scream for him to stop, pulling the trigger and painting the door crimson.

Derek vomited, one guard swore, the children screamed, and Hans Gerber stood there for a moment, gawking at his gruesome handiwork. The echoes ceased and he heard nothing. He saw nothing. Nothing but red. His heart stopped, his hand trembled.

Guilt, his old foe, threatened to end him right then. It commanded him to shove the gun to his own forehead and pull the trigger, but his instincts and a little devilish voice that sounded too much like Hitler whispered that it was fine. It was fine. It had to be fine. It was no worse than stepping on a bug.

A bug. He looked at the little girl's remains and forced himself to see nothing but a squashed bug, blurring his own vision until there was nothing but a blob of dirty Jew blood.

"There..." he whispered, pressing the gun against Derek's forehead. "There's my conviction."

He pulled the trigger, and Vilém, quite literally unable to stomach another moment, threw the stuffed cat to the floor. He bolted out of the nursery, out of Barrack One, and vomited in the mud.

"Fuck..." he gagged. He understood now why Joseph Klammer had refrained from showing him his own killings. The sensation of being a murderer was horrific, and worse...the justifications. The fight that took place in the Nazi's soul, the feeling of evil winning.

Winning! Vilém cursed himself for running when he realized he had fallen right into the Nazi's trap. Gerber had wanted to scare him, to drive him away, to make him into a coward.

"Not happening..." Vilém snarled. He didn't care what horrific things the Nazi insisted on showing him. He would not run away. He would not give the Nazi the satisfaction of frightening an undesirable.

Vilém marched back inside, back into the nursery. He looked down and saw that he had left his family album sitting open beside the toy cat. He saw little Fabian sitting on Sam's shoulders, grinning from ear to ear, and he wanted to sit and stare at that lovely image for hours, stare at it until the vision of the little girl vanished from his mind.

But no, no, that would be wrong. Ignoring her pain would be just as bad as forgetting Raya and all the rest.

Vilém sat down once more, cradling the cat in the crook of his arm and setting the album in his lap, bathing in Fabian's smile for only a moment before shutting his eyes.

You came back.

"You sound surprised, murderer."

I am not a murderer. Murder is killing a person...

"Isaac wasn't a person?"

People have pet rats.

"I felt what you felt back then, Hansie," said Vilém. "You can't pretend with me. Derek was right. You shot her because you were angry and afraid, afraid your little guards would tattle to Heydrich. And then when your conscience tried to guilt you into ending your pointless life, you freaked out and forced yourself to believe it. I bet you did that a thousand times until you actually started believing the bullshit."

It's not bullshit...but it was pointless.

"Hm?"

We lost, don't you get it? We did what we did for the greater good, we did...inhumane things...to better the world. And yet we lost. Everything we did was for nothing.

"Is that it, then? You just don't want all your murdering to be pointless?"

No...there's nothing else to be done. The war is over. The war against the Jews? Even if it continues in other forms, our cause is over. But...during the war...after what happened with Derek...I kept marching on, hoping that it would all be for a greater purpose, and hoping that I would find Isaac while doing this good work. But...well, you know that Heydrich eventually became the Reich-

sprotektor of Czechoslovakia. I could speak Czech, and therefore he took me with him.

"Well, Hans, I have good news and bad news."

Gerber strutted into a new memory, his chest weighed down with medals that Vilém could only assume he had received for shooting an appreciable amount of Jews.

Hans approached a large oaken desk that was covered in papers. He glanced at the reports and several words—*Transport, Solution, Effective*—leapt out at him, but most of it appeared to be bureaucratic blabber, albeit genocidal bureaucratic blabber.

Heydrich scribbled an untidy signature onto one document and plopped his pen into an inkwell, leaning back and cracking his knuckles as though the act of writing a death warrant was as taxing as beating an opponent.

"Good news first?" Hans pleaded, and Heydrich barely hid a smirk.

"You're getting a promotion. In fact, you're getting a new position," the Butcher of Prague declared. "We're streamlining the Final Solution, and since the plague is so spread out, we will need a precise network of camps and ghettos. We need a system to separate the Jews that can be put to work from the useless ones. The elderly, the sick...the children."

He paused for a moment, as though waiting for Hans to object to something he had said. When his underling remained complacently quiet, he gave a small nod of approval and continued.

"And since you've demonstrated your dedication to

the Cause, I think you've earned an opportunity. You will command a transit camp. You will have full control over every undesirable that enters your grounds. Consider yourself the Führer of the Camp. You've offered me loyalty, and therefore I will give you freedom."

"Thank you, Reichsprotektor!" said Hans. "I won't disappoint."

"I'm sure you won't," Heydrich muttered, picking up a folder and peeking at the contents therein with a small grimace.

"So...bad news now?" Heydrich said, looking at Hans like a father that had just hit the family dog with his car and wasn't sure how to explain himself. Gerber nodded and Heydrich leaned over the desk, offering the folder to his subordinate.

"I'm...sorry," the Hangman said, spitting out the words as though they stung his tongue. "It appears your *Edeljude* didn't survive. Died in a ghetto within the Sudetenland a year ago. Records were sparse, but we were able to confirm that this is...*was* him."

Hans' heart dropped to the bottom of his stomach, and he hesitated to open the folder. Morbid curiosity made him peek. There was a picture inside. Isaac Goldstein was indeed shown lying atop a pile of bodies, emaciated and filthy, his curly hair matted into a rat's nest, a stream of blood oozing from his lips.

Vilém had never felt someone's soul die so quickly. Whatever good there was within Hans Gerber perished right then, when he saw his almost-brother dead by Hitler's hands. His father's death had been for nothing.

Vilém felt bitter affection bloom in Hans' soul for a brief moment before it was beaten to death by his ego. He had loved Isaac, but Isaac was gone. There was nothing left except the Cause. Heydrich's Cause.

"He was only a dirty Jew," Hans said, tossing the folder back onto Heydrich's desk, and though Vilém expected Heydrich to approve of this sentiment, the Hangman of Prague raised a concerned eyebrow.

"You went through so much trouble to find him...*I* went through so much trouble to find him," Heydrich said. "He can't be that...disposable..."

But before Heydrich could say another word, he suddenly grunted and almost fell on top of his desk, as though something had kicked him square in the chest. Hans stepped back, and Vilém felt bewilderment buzz in the Nazi's brain.

"I don't suppose you believed in ghosts..." Vilém said.

I didn't believe in anything except the Cause.

"Well...I guess Heydrich probably had a lot of ghosts who wanted to kick his ass," Vilém remarked.

Perhaps. At the time, I just thought he was insane.

"He *was* insane," Vilém huffed, and insane though he may have been, Heydrich quickly recovered from whatever had made him spasm.

"Sorry...old injury acting up," Heydrich said, gesturing to his side. "What I *meant* to say was...don't...let this stand between you and your work. I would hate for you to go the way of that Derek fellow."

"I won't, Herr Heydrich, though I am curious...by any chance, did he leave behind a family? Children? I haven't seen him since 1930, he may have..."

"Fortunately, your *Edeljude* did not bring any more of his kind into the world," Heydrich sneered. "It appears he died as he lived: a worthless drunk."

Hans curled his hands into fists and nodded. "Very well."

"Understand, Gerber: your father's death in the Great War will not be meaningless. The work we are doing now, that work will avenge him. That work will make all the deaths in that war *and* this war worthwhile. We will make the world a utopia. *You* will. You will become your father's legacy. Work hard, get married, have plenty of Aryan children...let this Jew's death be your liberation, and continue to help us liberate the rest of the world."

Heydrich chuckled. "Sorry...I'm not as good at speeches as the Führer or Herr Goebbels, but...I do mean it."

"Thank you, Herr Heydrich," said Hans, his heart swelling with purpose. "You're completely correct...and if I may say, more persuasive than Herr Goebbels."

"Oh, get out of here!" Heydrich chuckled, waving for Hans to leave. "I'll have no bootlicking in my office. Go, go see your new kingdom."

"Yes, sir!" cried Hans, clicking his heels together, pulling his heart back into its proper place, and throwing his arm into the air. "Heil Hitler!"

And from that day on...well, I tried my hardest to live by Heydrich's words. But women were boring to me...

"Uhm..."

Not like that. I simply had no interest in being married, no lustful fantasies. I suppose I've always been practical. I didn't want to be a father either. Children are so...unpredictable. Look at Klaus Heydrich: his father was the Man with the Iron Heart, and he became a soft-hearted Jew-lover.

"God forbid your child have humanity," grumbled Vilém.

Regardless, I didn't like the odds. Instead, I threw myself into my work, the Cause. It went well, all things considered. The Camp you stand in was a model of efficiency for years. I was very hands-on, working from dawn 'till dusk, sorting Jews and making sure production was always at peak.

Eventually, I decided to move to the Camp, refurbishing the barrack you stand in for my own personal use. I even took up my old photography hobby once more. I was hoping that one day, when the Reich ruled over Europe and the Jews were an extinct race...well, I hoped that my pictures would show future generations how it was done. The iron will that was required. I hoped they would end up in a museum.

"Well...you got that much," Vilém snarked.

Yes, well...the world we sought to build never formed, but at the time I thought it was a certainty. We would win. We...we had to win. To make it all worth it, as Heydrich said. All of it...the Jews, their children, even my father. But although my work for the Cause consumed my life, I couldn't help but continue to think of Isaac.

"Need more albums..." A new memory formed. Kommandant Gerber sat at his desk with an enormous pile of leather albums sorted before him and a small stack of what appeared to be freshly developed photographs waiting to be catalogued.

Vilém shivered when he saw the picture at the top of the stack: a Nazi aiming a rifle at a woman who had collapsed while working. The Kommandant took the gruesome photo and opened one album, which was full of similar images. Dead Jews, injured Jews, smiling Nazis. Page after page of war crimes, so many pictures that he didn't have any room in the album for more.

He flipped through several more albums, searching for a space. When he found nothing, he opened a desk drawer and searched for another album, finding one at the bottom of his desk, an old brown book. The Nazi set the album on his desk and opened it.

His soul froze when he realized what he had uncovered. An old family album, filled with post-WWI pictures of little Hans Gerber and Isaac Goldstein.

Vilém could feel bile rise in Hans' throat, the ghost of his guilt threatening to haunt him. For a moment, he couldn't help but look down at the old memories. His eyes lingered on one picture of Isaac and himself as children sitting in front of a Christmas tree, leaning close, both hugging still-wrapped presents. Hans' gift was noticeably larger than Isaac's, yet it seemed that little Isaac hadn't yet realized how unfair everything was. He embraced his tiny box and grinned.

Hans stared at Isaac's bright, happy eyes for a moment. His own eyes began to sting, regret weighing down his heart.

A screech brought him back to his senses. He looked out the window and saw that a new train had arrived, filled with fresh undesirables to sort. He stood up, glanced back down at Isaac, and slammed the book shut. He grabbed his camera and rushed out of his office, fleeing from his not-brother's image.

Gerber ran out of Barrack One, which was being remodeled by several weary prisoners. He glanced at the Jews, smirking when they winced as he passed them by. He paused to snap a picture of the Jews painting over the old Barrack One sign and then strutted towards the Selection Platform. He arrived just in time to see the cattle-car doors slide open, and Vilém felt ill as eager interest took hold of the Nazi's mind, as though he had just walked into a new zoo exhibit.

"Good morning, Herr Kommandant," one Nazi soldier said. "Good batch today, fresh from the Sudetenland. Mostly Germans."

Hans turned to the young guard with a scolding scowl, and the Nazi hastily corrected himself.

"Jews who speak German," he stuttered, and the Kommandant nodded.

"No such thing as German Jews," he reminded his subordinate. "Get to it!"

"Yes, sir!" the Nazi cried, turning his furious attention onto the Jews.

"Men to the left, women to the right, children under fourteen form a separate group! Children under eleven must be surrendered to be cared for in the nursery!"

"Here we go!" whispered Hans, lifting his up his camera and frantically snapping pictures as chaos erupted on the Platform. Jews tumbled out of the train cars and were yanked from their children before they even got a chance to say goodbye. Those who were too ill to move were shoved and beaten by the Nazis. Some people had died on the train, and their family members tried in vain to get them help while the Kapos carried their bodies to the Pit. The Selection was deafening. Wailing children, sobbing women, shouting Nazis, barking dogs.

Hans couldn't take photos fast enough. *Snap, snap, snap!* He tried to capture as many moments of terror as he could. One Nazi sicced a dog on a man who was refusing to leave his children. The Kommandant snickered, raising his camera and snapping away, as though he was on a safari and was watching a lion tear a gazelle to bits. The man's children bawled, but another Nazi grabbed them and dragged them away. They were far too young to be of any use to the Reich as slave labor. They would go to the Pit with the rest of the babies.

Vilém wanted to vomit again. He had seen the Selection too many times, but in every other memory he had experienced it through the eyes of the victims—save, of course, for Joseph Klammer, but the repentant Nazi had viewed the whole affair with disgust. Kommandant Gerber regarded it with delight.

Feeling the joy in the Kommandant's chest, the excitement, while dogs tore people to shreds and families were ripped apart...to hear these screams and feel nothing but satisfaction...it was sickening. It made Vilém's head hurt.

"He's eleven! He just looks little for his age!"

"He is not eleven, lying Jewish whore!"

The Kommandant turned just in time to see a Nazi

slap a woman so hard she fell to the ground. Her son, whom she had been trying to protect, clung to her. He was obviously younger than eleven, five or six years old at most, and...

In unison, Vilém and the Kommandant were struck by a bolt of familiarity. The boy had curly ebony hair, soft blue eyes. Vilém released a shuddering breath, his heart pounding, but he kept his revelation to himself.

"Isaac...?" Kommandant Gerber whispered. Though the child didn't look exactly like Isaac Goldstein, the similarities were too numerous to be a coincidence.

One Nazi grabbed the little boy, pulling him away from his injured mother, carrying him towards the Pit with all the other useless young children.

"Wait!" Kommandant Gerber yelled, almost dropping his camera as he ran to the boy. The soldier stopped, holding the kicking, squealing child with both arms and regarding his boss with a raised eyebrow. The child's mother looked up at the Kommandant with a tiny dash of hope in her eyes.

"Herr, please!" she cried, grabbing Gerber's pant leg. "He's old, he can work, he can..."

"I don't care about that," grunted the Kommandant, pulling his leg out of her grasp and pushing her away with his jackboot. "Who is the boy's father?"

"His father was a German, sir..."

"His name, do you know his father's name?"

"It was Isaac Goldstein, sir, please, I...he wasn't even a Jew, his father..."

"That's a lie," snarled the Kommandant, turning away from the boy's mother and letting his eyes settle on

Isaac's son. The boy had stopped struggling. He was watching the Kommandant with wide, inquisitive eyes, perhaps sensing that something strange was going on.

"I'm sorry, sir, please forgive me..." sobbed the mother.

"Were you married to Isaac Goldstein?" grunted Hans. "Tell me about him."

"He...he was a good man, but...he had problems with alcohol. We were never married...I loved him, but he left when our son was little and I don't know what became of him."

"The boy is definitely his, then?"

"Y-yes, sir...uhm...did you know Isaac?"

The Kommandant didn't answer. Too many feelings were clashing in his chest as he looked at Isaac's only son. Affection for his not-brother, an instinct to protect the last piece of him...but he had trained himself to be disgusted by Jews for so many years that hatred tried its best to batter love into submission.

He hesitated for a moment, letting the war rage in his soul until, at last, love won.

"The boy will not be harmed," he declared, striding towards his soldier and opening his arms. The Nazi handed the child to his boss, and the Kommandant started to carry the boy back to Barrack One.

"Wait, where are you taking him?!" the mother screamed, and Isaac's son started fighting again.

"Let me go! Mama! Mama!" the child screeched, and the Kommandant grunted in ire, glancing over his shoulder.

"Take care of her," he commanded his men, nudging

his head to indicate the mother, and without another word he carried the howling, writhing boy back to his unfinished home.

I couldn't let him die...I thought that perhaps, even though Isaac's life was pointless, a waste...perhaps this child could be trained, raised as a German. Perhaps he could forget his origins and have a good life in the New World, with a new identity...

"You stole him from his people, from his mother!" hissed Vilém.

I saved him! He would have gone right to the Pit with all the other children!

"Because *you* would have sent him there!" Vilém argued. "Heydrich said you were king of the Camp. You could have spared all the children if you wanted to!"

And waste valuable food and medicine on useless eaters? No. But for Isaac, and for my father, I took the boy in. I gave him a new life.

"Please hold still."

"I want to see my mother..."

"You may see her, but only if you hold still."

A new memory started, though they hadn't jumped too far forward in time. Isaac's son was cleaned, wearing a Hitler Youth uniform and resting in a bare room that Vilém realized was going to become his nursery. He was sitting on a stool while the Kommandant dyed his inky hair gold, making him look like a little Aryan.

"So curly, just like Isaac's..." muttered the Kommandant as he painted the black locks blonde.

"You knew my father?" the boy queried, and the Kommandant smiled.

"I did."

"He was drunk and horrible," the child sighed, crossing his arms and pouting. The Kommandant couldn't help but laugh.

"I can't argue with that, but you're going to be better than him," Hans said. "From now on, you'll be German. You will have a very nice life."

"But I don't wanna be German, I'm Jewish and Czech..." the boy argued, and the Kommandant's smile vanished.

"That's too bad," he said. "If you want to see your mother, you have to be a good German boy. You may not speak Czech or Hebrew or Yiddish, and you may not practice any Jewish ceremony."

"But God says..."

"God does not exist," the Kommandant declared, giving the child's hair a slight tug to emphasize his point. "The notion is fanciful, and the Jewish religion is based on ancient nonsense. The Jewish people are a vile race..."

"I'm not vile!"

"No, and that's why I'd like to save you."

"And Mama too, right? Mama's not vile!"

"If you behave and do as you're told, your mother will not be harmed."

"Promise?"

"Yes. Now hold still, I'm almost done," the Kommandant said. With one final blot of dye, he transformed the little Jew into an Aryan cherub. He stepped back and observed his work with a grin.

"There! Now don't you feel better?" he asked. The boy's shoulders sagged and he kicked his legs anxiously.

"It feels wrong," he confessed. "Mama says God wants Jews to be proud."

"Jews have nothing to be proud of," the Kommandant sneered. He picked up his camera and grabbed the boy by the hand. As he pulled him off the stool, however, the child's sleeve slid upwards, revealing an enormous bruise covering his entire forearm. The child seemed unaffected by the sight of the huge black blotch, but the Kommandant immediately released the boy, worry filling his heart.

"What happened?" he asked. "Did you get that on the train?"

"Nah ah, when the Nazi grabbed me on the Platform," the boy said.

"That's impossible. He was only a little rough with you, he didn't beat you."

"I'm a hemo-fil-a-ac," the boy said, slowly pronouncing the word, which his mother must have trained him to say many a time. "My body's weird and if I get a little bump or a cut, it's like I'm about to die."

"You're not acting like you're about to die," observed the Kommandant, gently rolling up the boy's other sleeve and wincing when he saw another massive bruise.

"I get unlucky a lot, and I'm used to hurting," the boy said. The Kommandant nodded, dragging the boy's sleeves over the wounds.

"I see...well, I'll have to make sure you're not injured, then..." he muttered.

"Herr Kommandant," the boy said. "I thought it was against the law for a Jew to say he's a German. Isn't it illegal?"

"Hush!" hissed the Kommandant, lightly tapping the boy's cheek. "That is precisely why you must never say you're a Jew or behave like one. If you do, I will get in trouble and you and your mother will suffer. Come, we have to get your new identity card printed..."

He ushered the boy to a blank wall and had him stand against it.

"Your new name will be Martin Gerber the Second," the Kommandant said, and the boy scowled.

"But my name is..."

"Martin!" barked the Kommandant. "Your name is Martin! You are German! Be grateful for that. You will not be killed as a Jew, but your life as a Jew is over." He raised the camera.

"Smile!" he commanded. The boy refused, crossing his arms.

"I don't feel like smilin'..." he whispered. The Kommandant let out an irate growl.

"You *are* your father's son," he grumbled. "Be a good boy and do as you're told. Germans do as they are told; you are a German now."

"*You're* not doing what you're told," Little Martin argued. "You're not supposed to be doing this with me, I know that."

The Kommandant could not help but smile. "Fine, frown if you like. I guess it doesn't matter."

He pressed his eye against the viewfinder and snapped a photograph.

I will admit...I liked Martin. He was like a better version of Isaac. He reminded me of what Isaac was like when we were children. He was smart, studious, and polite. I was sure he would have a good future, and I did my best to give him everything a German boy could ever want.

"Martin! Come here! I have a surprise for you!"

A new memory started up. Vilém could feel the Kommandant clutching something small and stuffed in his hand as he entered his hearth. Little Martin came running, his eyes bright and eager.

"What is it?!" the child squealed, coming to a halt in front of the Kommandant, who examined the boy with a grimace of disapproval.

"Now, Martin, what have we talked about?" he chastised, and the boy's smile wilted. Martin submissively bowed his head and raised up a limp arm.

"Heil Hitler..." he grumbled through gritted teeth. The Kommandant regarded this proper German greeting with an approving smile, ruffling the boy's dyed hair.

"Much better, you'll get it," the Kommandant said. "I went to town and look what I got you!"

He held the gift out towards the boy, a small stuffed bear. The boy's optimism faded and he took the toy with a disappointed frown.

"Oh...another toy," Martin sighed. "Thank you, Kommandant."

"Look on the bottom!" the Kommandant said. "I had it monogrammed just for you. You should keep it on your bed instead of that old toy cat."

Vilém gripped the little cat tighter. Martin looked at the bear's rump and bit his lip when he saw the initials: "M.G."

"Thank you..." Martin mumbled. "I like my toy cat, though...Mama gave it to me."

The child put harsh emphasis on the word "Mama" and looked up at the Kommandant with a plea screaming in his baby blue eyes. Kommandant Gerber felt his chest tighten.

"I know you want to see your mother," he said, his tone icy. "But you must learn patience. You have been given a lot, and your mother is busy. You must be grateful for what you have."

"I am grateful, sir..."

"Good boy. Then let's not speak of this any longer. Have you finished your homework for the day?"

"I don't like my homework..." the child muttered, and though the Kommandant laughed, Vilém could feel aggravation boil in the Nazi's chest.

"Few children do! But your education is important. Come, let's see what you have so far."

The Kommandant started marching towards the nursery, Martin trodding behind him. The formerly bare room was now filled with toys of every sort. A train set, a stack of board games, and stuffed animals of every species.

See? So spoiled...and yet he insisted on keeping that little toy cat. Had me go all the way to the sorting barrack so he could get it back...

Martin set the new bear beside his favorite toy, the much cheaper and clearly beloved stuffed cat that Vilém was clutching.

"It meant something to him," Vilém said. "His

mother gave it to him and you wouldn't let him see her...what happened to her?"

What happened? What do you think happened? I told my men to take care of her.

"Oh," Vilém seethed. "So you lied to him...and you murdered his mother."

His mother was a Jewess. She would have been a bad influence on him. I was trying to make him into a proper German. I worked very hard to make sure he was well educated.

The boy shuffled to a small desk that rested in the corner by the bed, grabbing a slip of paper off it and sheepishly handing his assignment to the Kommandant. Gerber read over the child's sloppy answers.

"Let's see how you've done in math. 'If a boy has one full German father, but his mother is half German and half Czech, what percent of the boy is racially pure?' Oh, Martin, you got it wrong. One hundred percent? It would only be seventy-five percent."

"General Heydrich says some Czechs can be Aryans," Martin argued, and the Kommandant chuckled.

"Clever boy, using my boss against me! Very well, I'll have to write out less controversial questions. Let's see...number two. 'To keep an invalid alive costs four Reichsmarks a day. At an asylum where one hundred inmates are held, how much does it cost a productive German citizen to keep them all alive for merely a single day?' Very good, Martin, four hundred a day! And that's only for one asylum!"

"Thank you, Kommandant..." muttered the boy, sitting on the bed and looking down at his feet. He reached out and hugged his favorite toy cat to his chest. When the Kommandant saw the child's obvious demonstration of nervousness, his pride petered into nothingness. He read the last question.

"'Two Germans enter a room, followed by two Jews. If one German leaves, how many people are left in the room?' Oh...silly boy. Three people are left in the room? No, only one person would be left in the room. One person and two subhumans. It's a bit of a trick question, I suppose..."

"These don't feel like math problems," whispered Martin, squeezing his toy cat. "And I'm a person."

"Naturally, you're a person, Martin," said the Kommandant, feigning a casual tone even as Vilém felt Hans' heart hammering with agitation. "You're a German."

"But I'm a J..."

"Hush!" snapped the Kommandant, and Vilém could tell that if the boy were not a hemophiliac and the Kommandant weren't afraid that a bit of corporal punishment could kill him, he would have smacked Martin across the face. Instead, he merely covered the boy's mouth with one gloved hand.

"We have talked about this, Martin," he hissed. "You want to see your mother again, don't you?"

"Y...yes..." hiccupped Martin, tears falling from his eyes, his cracking voice muffled by the Nazi's palm.

"Jews don't get to see their mothers. Good German boys get what they want. Good German boys who listen and obey and do their homework properly get everything they want. Now..."

He held up the homework sheet. "How many people are in the room?"

The child hesitated to dehumanize the people he belonged to, the people he loved, but his eyes flitted down to the little cat and the small hope that he could see his mother again made him whimper, "One."

Satisfaction and relief flowed through the Kommandant's bloodstream. He handed the boy his homework sheet and patted his head. "Good boy."

Normally, he was pliant as long as I dangled his mother in front of him. I hoped with time and isolation from the other members of his race, he would accept his new identity. But he always returned to Jewish nonsense, and it was easy for him to do so. His condition meant that he had to have a doctor nearby at all times, and naturally I couldn't have a German doctor stay in my house.

"Naturally," Vilém huffed. "He might have tattled to Heydrich."

Precisely. Too many private conversations were held in this building. I could only have undesirable doctors service him, and most doctors who arrived at the Camp were Jews. I warned them not to speak to Martin about Jewish matters, but so many didn't listen. We went through a lot of doctors...

"Martin, what is this?"

A new memory started, and Vilém could feel the Kommandant's heart pounding with fury and panic as he stormed into the nursery, two SS men flanking him. Martin had been sitting at his desk, doing another "math assignment", but when he saw the Kommandant, he dropped his pencil.

"What is...?" the boy stuttered, and the Kommandant unfolded a crumpled piece of paper.

"I found this in your trash," he snapped. He glanced at the scrap page and Vilém realized the paper was filled with Hebrew letters.

"K-Kommandant, please...I...I'll be a better Nazi if I know how to speak to Jews!" the boy cried, dropping to his knees in front of the Kommandant.

"By the time you're grown up, there won't be any Jews to communicate with," the Kommandant sneered, tearing the paper in two and dropping the halves in front of the boy. "Your doctor gave you Hebrew lessons."

"Please don't hurt him, he just did what I asked!" screamed the child, wrapping his arms around the Kommandant's leg, tears streaming down his rosy cheeks. "Please, please!"

"Consider this a lesson, boy," the Kommandant snapped, gesturing for his men to enter the infirmary. The two SS men did as commanded and kicked down the door, dragging an old Jewish doctor out. Not Doctor Doubek. One of his unfortunate predecessors. The doctor screamed and begged for his life.

"I'm sorry, I'm sorry!" the doctor yelled, and Martin, bawling, tried to run towards the doctor, tried to defend him with his little body, but the Kommandant was quick. He scooped the boy into his arms.

"Stay calm, child," the Kommandant whispered in the boy's ear. "You've already misbehaved. Keep struggling and you won't be allowed to see your mother for another month."

But Little Martin, too concerned for the fate of his

doctor, disobeyed, struggling and reaching for the prisoner as the two SS guards beat him. The doctor's blood splattered across the cushioned floor.

"Stop it, stop it, he didn't do anything wrong! Please! I wanna be punished instead!" screamed Martin, kicking the Kommandant in the gut. Gerber grunted, and Vilém felt his anger spike.

"Just take care of the fucking Jew!" he snapped at his men. "Take it out back and put it out of its misery!"

"Don't kill him, please, please!" screeched Martin. Vilém thought he might have to drop the cat again. The doctor, praying for mercy, was dragged out of the nursery. Martin was fighting, the Kommandant's soul was burning with hatred and ire, the child kept kicking and howling until...

BANG!

A gunshot echoed from outside, and the Kommandant dropped the child to the floor.

"Now," sighed the Kommandant, massaging his sore chest. "Next time, when I tell you not to seek out Jewish..."

But before he could say another word, Little Martin ran to his metal bedpost.

"I hate you, I hate you, I hate you!" the boy screamed, punctuating every pronouncement by slamming his head against the edge of the bedpost. The Kommandant watched the child self-harm, frozen with surprise, but after the boy struck himself so hard that Barrack One trembled, he came to his senses and intervened.

"Martin, stop! Martin, stop it!" he cried, grabbing the

child and pulling him away from the bedpost. The boy had pierced his skin, and the minor gash he had created was gushing blood. The Kommandant grabbed a random stuffed animal, a smiling turtle, and shoved it against the boy's forehead in a desperate attempt to stem the flow.

"Stupid boy!" he snarled as the child's blood turned the emerald turtle scarlet. "Stupid little Jew!"

The memory shifted. Martin was lying down on the bed, his head wrapped in crimson-blotched bandages, hugging his little cat. The Kommandant stood above him, scowling.

"You shouldn't have done that, Martin..." he sighed. "You might have killed yourself."

"You killed my doctor," Martin countered, not daring to glower directly at the Kommandant, instead directing all of his anger at the roof.

"Martin..."

"Don't kill my doctors if you don't want me to die."

"I'll get you a new doctor, but you can't ask them to teach you about Judaism anymore. It's not my fault, I warned you what would happen. It's your fault."

The boy trembled, squeezing his eyes shut and turning his back to the Kommandant.

"I know..." he whimpered.

"Do not ask them again and no harm will befall them. And do not purposefully injure yourself."

"Why not?" the child hissed, his little voice cracking with guilt and hatred.

"You know you're very important to me, Martin," sighed the Kommandant, patting the child's back. The boy shrunk away from his touch.

"I want my mama..." the child sobbed.

"You didn't listen before, Martin. I warned you. You don't behave, you don't get to see your mother. One month. No mother. Be good and do your assignments and maybe I'll reconsider."

The boy hiccupped and nodded, still refusing to face the Nazi. Kommandant Gerber's heart reared up in fury.

"Martin, be a good boy and look at me," he commanded. "Good German boys are polite and grateful."

Vilém could see disgust hold the boy back, but love for his mother made him swallow his pride again. He turned to face the Kommandant, his cheeks red and stained with tears, his lips trembling.

"Yes, sir..." he said.

"Good boy. I'm going back to work now, say goodbye the right way."

The boy whimpered as though the Kommandant had told him to commit the unholiest sin.

"Martin..." the Kommandant warned, reaching out and putting a hand on the boy's cat. "Bad little Jews don't get to have toys."

Loathing glowed in the child's eyes, but he tightened his grip on the cat and obeyed, lifting up one little hand and squeaking, "Heil Hitler."

"Jesus Christ!" Vilém spat. "You *are* a monster!"

I was trying to keep the boy alive, to give him a better life...

"You *blamed him* for *you* murdering his friend!" snapped Vilém. "You lied to him about his mother to try and morph him into a little Nazi! How can you *not* see what a shitbag you are?"

I genuinely don't understand. You're supposed to be seeing things from my point of view...

"Yes! And even from your point of view, you're a terrible human being!" cried Vilém. "It is *astonishing* how many hoops you're jumping through to continue to think you're a good person. Fuck! Even Heydrich let Iveta Sladký live, you didn't even spare the child's mother!"

I would argue that makes Heydrich a hypocrite. What is worse? Someone who follows his principles, or someone who bends them where it's convenient?

"You bent them too—you took in a Jew and gave him a fake ID! That was illegal! That was a violation of your so-called principles!"

Oh, I'm sure Heydrich would have said the same. Cold-hearted bastard didn't understand the difference between making my father's sacrifice worthwhile and letting his brat son keep a pet Jew. Nevertheless...I did owe him for the relative freedom he offered me. And besides, I hoped that an Aryan-looking Jew like little Fido...

"Iveta!" snarled Vilém. "At the very least say her real name."

You undesirables are so picky about your names. Fine, Iva or whatever her name was. She moved into the house, and I hoped that Little Martin would at least brighten up if he had a supposedly Aryan playmate. But while he played with her, he didn't like her very much. And when-

ever Heydrich would bring his little brat over to visit, Martin would be miserable.

"Gerber, I didn't think your boy would be so shy. Don't tell me he's afraid of being beaten by a little girl! Worse, a little Jewess."

Again, a new memory formed, and a familiar high-pitched voice made both Vilém and the Kommandant's chests tighten with aggravation. The Kommandant sat on the edge of his desk holding a half-empty bottle of beer. Heydrich was leaning by the open window, looking down into the garden. The Kommandant set his drink aside and slowly sauntered over, standing beside his mentor and peering outside.

Klaus Heydrich and Iveta Sladký were having a ball: both had taken up arms in the form of wooden swords and were engaged in a brutal duel. They laughed, a sweet sound that made Gerber feel like vomiting.

"See? He's by the doghouse. Why do you have that, by the way? You don't have a dog," Heydrich pointed out.

Gerber didn't answer. He glanced at Iveta's doghouse. Little Martin was sitting against the dilapidated structure, his back to the other children, anger etched onto his face as he stubbornly hugged his toy cat.

"Poor kid," Vilém muttered. Martin had no clue that Iveta was a Jew and Klaus was nothing like his father. If only he had known...perhaps they could have been friends, perhaps he could have had some moments of happiness at the Camp.

But Martin could only see Fido the Nazi Spy and Heydrich's little prince. He hid from them as though he was afraid they would start beating him with their wooden swords.

"I *told* him to play nice..." muttered the Kommandant, and Heydrich shrugged, taking a casual sip of his beer.

"Boys will rarely do as they are told. I love my sons, but my daughter is much easier to deal with. By the way, you should find a dog for that doghouse. Boys need pets, it teaches them to take responsibility. Klaus has our dog, some chickens that Himmler gave us, and I gave him his own horse just this year after our other dog died, poor Daxi..."

"And he has a pet Jew," the Kommandant snarked. Heydrich turned to his accomplice with a cold warning in his eyes.

"I'm joking," the Kommandant said hastily. "Klaus is too sweet for his own good."

"Yes..." muttered Heydrich. The Hangman realized his son had paused his duel with Iveta and was slowly approaching Martin. Klaus Heydrich gingerly tapped Martin's shoulder with the point of his sword. When Martin turned with a start, the younger Heydrich offered the sword to him.

Martin shook his head, clinging ever tighter to the cat. Klaus frowned with disappointment and his arm flopped to his side in defeat. Heydrich's son seemed to sense that he was being watched and looked up, his eyes locking with his father's. Gerber smirked as what little color remained in General Heydrich's cheeks drained away.

For a moment, they stood there in silence, Iveta

watching the standoff with terror, Kommandant Gerber with amusement. If Heydrich didn't feel guilty about this entire affair, he at the very least felt embarrassed. Klaus broke first by raising up a hand and giving a tiny wave, a wave that his father slowly returned. Klaus offered his father a slight smile, then gestured with his sword towards Iveta.

"Go on..." Heydrich mouthed, motioning for his son to have fun. Klaus' eyes brightened with hope, and Vilém felt a stab of pity for the boy. He must have thought there was something good left in his father, some small sliver of kindness. He returned to Iveta with a bounce in his step.

Kommandant Gerber, whose chest was about to explode with anger, saw a teeny smile tease the corner of Heydrich's lips and he couldn't help but snap, "You're not being a good father, Reinhard."

Heydrich turned to face the Kommandant, raising an eyebrow and gesturing for him to elaborate. Gerber pointed at Iveta.

"You let your child associate with a Jew. Continue to do this and he will not be able to exist within the new world we're creating."

"Is that a threat?" Heydrich hissed.

"Not at all, but you're teaching him to have affection for a race we are going to exterminate. What will you do when he's older? What if he defects? Resists? Becomes an enemy of the state? It's not safe. It's *dangerous*. Were I you, I would have ignored his pleas, given him discipline..."

"I don't hit my children, Kommandant. I know you don't hit yours either."

"There are other ways to control a child besides physical force," the Kommandant argued, and Heydrich's face darkened.

"I know..." the Blonde Beast muttered.

"My point is, however you chose to deal with your son's misbehavior, you should have had the Jewess put down."

"I understand your argument, Hans," sighed Heydrich, glancing down at the glistening Nazi pin on his breast. "But you know as well as I do that when you love someone, you will bend politics for their safety and happiness."

"The Jewish Question goes far beyond politics, General Heydrich, as *you* taught me," the Kommandant snapped, an accusatory edge in his tone. "Besides, as far as I was *told*, the purpose of doing this work to solve the Jewish Question is to preserve our children's safety and happiness. Reichsprotektor, you might as well let your son keep a poisonous snake as a pet."

"You know, I don't take the Bible seriously," Heydrich sneered. "But I feel like you're 'casting the first stone', Hans. If I recall, you had your own *Edeljude* you wanted to protect."

"Well, maybe I was wrong!" the Kommandant hissed. "Why is it all right for you or I or Klaus to have an *Edeljude?* The average German does not get to keep their one good Jew, and I was under the impression that all Germans are equal under the Führer."

"If we let *every* German keep his good Jew, we would never solve the Jewish Problem..."

"But then *is there* a Jewish Problem?!" the Kommandant finally cried, and Vilém felt Hans' instincts scream for him to stop, beg him to take that back. He was questioning too much. It was dangerous.

But the dam was broken and he let his doubts out. "If *every* Jew has some upstanding German citizen willing to vouch for them—maybe not *every* Jew, but most German Jews—if that's the case, is there really a Jewish Question at all?"

Vilém expected Heydrich the so-called perfect Nazi to rebuke Hans like a priest might an altar boy who dared to question Church doctrine. He was surprised when the Blonde Beast's icy eyes warmed and he reached up, closing one gloved hand around his Nazi Party pin.

"You know..." Heydrich whispered. "Sometimes I wonder about that."

His grip tightened around the pin, as though there was a small part of him, the pinprick of goodness that Klaus could still see, that wanted to rip the pin off and stop the madness right then. The Kommandant watched his mentor, waiting...but Heydrich loosened his grip and brushed his thumb against the swastika.

"I guess it's too late to really ask those questions now...isn't it?" Heydrich said, and the Kommandant looked out at the Camp, at the ash-filled Pit, at the bodies of starved prisoners piled high in the distance.

"Yes..." Hans whispered, bowing his head.

"We've gone too far," Heydrich decreed, his high-pitched voice somehow rising an octave. "We *have* to finish it. We *have* to be right. We *are* right. People like you and I, through our sacrifices, we have earned our exceptions. It isn't unfair. It isn't."

"No..." muttered the Kommandant, barely keeping his tone from wavering. Heydrich looked down at his own hand. There was a ring decorating one of his long, thin fingers, a ring shaped like a skull. He stared into the little skull's empty eyes for a moment before smiling bitterly.

"You know, Himmler was telling me the other day that he thinks when I'm gone, I should have all my medals and trinkets put in a museum. So my children and their children can see what I did and share it with the whole world."

He looked up, and if Vilém hadn't known the monster he was looking at, he might have felt pity for Heydrich right then. He had never seen a more uncertain face.

"What do you think, Gerber?" the Blonde Beast asked. "Do you want to be in a museum someday?"

"Ha!" laughed Vilém. "Well, Gerber, what do you think about your museum?"

I'm not fond of it, and I imagine if Heydrich could see his exhibit, he wouldn't like it either. But, well...he ended up becoming a martyr for the Cause.

"That 'martyr' sounded pretty sarcastic."

He didn't deserve one bit of the adoration he received. He was a pure hypocrite, and yet when he perished like a fool, the whole Reich was obligated to weep for him. Everyone...except one child...

"Kommandant Gerber!"

A new memory formed. Kommandant Gerber was standing before a large memorial that was drowning in wreaths and flowers. A bust of Heydrich sneered at him from the top of the memorial, and anger bubbled up in the Kommandant's belly.

"Kommandant Gerber!"

He turned and saw little Klaus, standing beside his younger brother and the head of the SS, Heinrich Himmler. Klaus broke away from his "Uncle" Himmler and darted towards the Kommandant. Gerber's anger elevated when he realized that the child was dry-eyed.

"Well, well, Klaus," he scoffed. "Aren't you putting on a brave face! You must be traumatized."

Klaus' eyes flitted towards his father's bust, and the Kommandant saw a strangely bitter smile flicker across the child's face.

"Boy, show your father some respect," the Kommandant hissed. "I assure you, if you were my son..."

"Thankfully, I'm not," Klaus declared, whipping an envelope out of his pocket and pushing it against the Kommandant's chest. "My father may be gone, but I can still make your life Hell if you hurt Iveta. Give this to her and keep her safe and happy."

"Ha! Well! Taking after your old man!" the Kommandant laughed, quickly pocketing the envelope. He shot a cautious look at Himmler, hoping he hadn't seen that exchange, but the Reichsführer of the SS was too busy comforting Klaus' brother to spot anything suspicious.

"I take after Papa enough to be nosy," Klaus said, crossing his arms behind his back, his lively blue eyes suddenly becoming icy, a smirk that seemed too much like his father's blooming on his boyish face.

"So..." the child said, his voice dropping to a whisper.

"How about you keep my Jew a secret and I won't tell my Godfather Himmler about yours?"

The Kommandant felt his heartbeat screech to a halt. He looked down at the insufferably snide child and barely suppressed the urge to deck the boy across the face.

"Martin told you?" he whispered. Klaus shook his head.

"I snooped. He writes things about you...he hates you, you know."

"You need to be quiet, boy..." snarled the Kommandant.

"So do you, *Kommandant*."

"I will not be ordered around by a dead General's brat...besides, you wouldn't say a word. You're softer than your father, Klaus, and you wouldn't want Martin's blood on your hands."

"Maybe..." Klaus said with a nod. "Are you gonna take that chance? You really shouldn't bet on a Heydrich being merciful."

"No...I suppose not."

"Good. I've gotta..." Klaus started to say, but the Kommandant suddenly reached out, grabbing the boy's wrist and pulling him back. The junior Heydrich turned with a look of disbelief, but his ire melted when he saw that the Kommandant's aggravation had morphed into dismay.

"What...did he write about me?" Hans asked. Klaus scowled, tugging his arm out of the Kommandant's grasp.

"What do you *think* he wrote?" Klaus snapped, retreating to Himmler's side without another word.

Heydrich's boy was right: I didn't want to test his mercy, so I kept Iveta around until he ended up getting splattered by a bus...but almost as soon as I got home from the funeral, I set out to find this secret journal Klaus had uncovered. You'll never guess where it was...

"He kept it in the cat," Vilém assumed, squeezing the old stuffed animal.

Correct! God knows how the little Heydrich brat figured it out so fast, I searched everywhere. But behind the button eye was a little hole, and in that little hole was a collection of papers. Letters.

"To who?"

His mother.

"'Mama, I hate every second of this, I hate to live a lie. Every time I say "Heil Hitler", it burns my tongue, but I will say it a million times to see you again. I pray to Adonai that I will see you soon and I pray that God sees all the evil in Gerber.'"

A new memory started, and the amount of fury that flowed through the Kommandant as he read the little boy's letter aloud was almost painful. Vilém was surprised that the boy was still breathing, much less unharmed. But the Kommandant stopped himself from striking the boy, instead pacing in front of Little Martin.

Martin sat on the end of his bed, hugging his now one-eyed toy cat and staring down at the cushioned floor. The boy's face was unreadable. He refused to show any sign of how afraid he truly was, but Vilém could see tears clinging to the corners of his eyes.

The Kommandant finished the note, tore it into tiny

pieces and hurled the shreds at the child, who winced as though acid rain was falling upon him.

"You really believe that about me?" Hans snapped. "After all I've done for you? After all I've given you...come here!"

He suddenly reached for the child, and Vilém was afraid he would grab Martin by the hair or wrist and seriously injure him. Fortunately, for as furious as the Kommandant was, he remembered Martin's condition and instead grabbed the little toy cat, knowing that the boy would refuse to let go of his most precious possession. Martin clung to the cat's tail and trotted behind the Kommandant, who gripped the toy's head and stomped all the way to the developing room.

"K-Kommandant!" Raya Pomnenka was busily hanging several pictures up on a wire. She paused her work and stood at attention, her head bowed, her burned hands at her sides. The Kommandant shoved her towards the door.

"Out, Pomnenka, go outside with Fido!" the Kommandant snarled. Raya didn't hesitate, scurrying past the Kommandant and the child, shooting the boy a sympathetic look as she fled. The Kommandant noticed this and slammed the door behind her, plunging the developing room into partial darkness.

"Does she know?" he barked, pointing towards the spot where Raya had been standing. "Does she know you're a Jew? Have you talked to her too?"

"No, no! I haven't told her or Fido!" screamed the boy, falling to his knees. "Please don't hurt anyone! Please! I'm sorry!"

"Why should I believe a word you say after you wrote horrible lies about me?" growled the Kommandant, dropping the cat and crossing his arms. "I bet you told her...I bet you told her, and if you did...she has to go. Nobody who knows you're a Jew can be allowed to live! You know why?"

"Yes, sir..."

"Say it, you ungrateful brat!"

"Because you care about me and you're my protector," whimpered the child, pressing the cat to his cheek as though he desperately wanted someone to give him a comforting kiss.

"Correct! You see these!" The Kommandant snatched several pictures off the wire, blurry black-and-white images of Jews at work, Jews starving, Jews burning...he grabbed the boy by the hair and forced him to look up, shoving the photos in his face.

"This! This is what will happen to you if anyone finds out! If you tell a soul! Look, look!" Hans commanded.

"You're hurting me!" Martin squealed, dropping his toy and grabbing the Kommandant's hands, trying to pry the Nazi's fingers off his hair. The Kommandant released the boy, sneering when he saw that a few golden splotches of dye were staining his gloves.

"I've given you a new life," the Kommandant said. "I saved you from this!"

He tossed the pictures at the boy, who ducked and covered as though the horrifying photos were bombs.

"If you hate this life so much, perhaps I should let you go back to living like a Jew!" suggested the Kommandant. "You and your mother can be reunited, and you both can go to the Pit! If I'm so evil..."

"Please don't kill me!" whimpered Martin. "Please, I'm sorry, you're right, you're right, I'm ungrateful..."

"Damn right!" snapped the Kommandant, stomping his foot beside the boy's head, making the floorboards creak and bend.

"Please don't hurt me, please!" wailed the boy.

"You, I won't...for now. But if you think I'm so evil, perhaps I should take away your doctor. And your mother, perhaps she should be sent away...after all, I am *evil*."

"You're not evil!" the boy lied, clinging to the Kommandant's foot. "You're not evil, please, I was being silly! Please don't hurt anyone! Please, please!"

The Kommandant looked down at the sobbing child with disdain, remaining silent for a moment before sneering, "It seems your lessons have not taken hold. Really, maybe I should let you play with Heydrich's boy more often. He at least knows that German boys do not *beg*."

He pulled his foot away from the boy and declared, "A German boy *demands*. So, Martin, *demand* that I spare your mother and perhaps I will. Because I am not evil, I will be merciful, but I want you to show me that there's some German spirit in you."

He waved for the boy to get to his feet, to demand like a true German. The child remained on his knees, however, and the Kommandant began to feel nervous when he saw realization flaring in Martin's eyes.

"A German doesn't beg," the child whispered. "And

ELYSE HOFFMAN

a Jew doesn't deserve mercy...and Germans never give what is not deserved..."

"It seems you *have* been listening to my lessons," the Kommandant mumbled, arching an eyebrow. "Come now, let's see..."

"You wouldn't spare my mother," the child said, slowly rising to his feet, his face twisting with anger. "You said it yourself! Anyone who knows I'm a Jew has to die, and my mother knows I'm a Jew!"

"Martin..." the Kommandant whispered, but the boy had figured it out. Martin lunged at the Kommandant, trying to shove him into the tub of chemicals behind him, screaming, kicking.

"You liar! You liar!" screeched the boy. "She's already dead! You liar! You never spared her! She's dead! She's dead! You killed her, you German bastard!"

"Martin, enough!" the Kommandant cried, grabbing the boy's wrists, having to keep a tight hold to prevent the boy from continuing his attack. The child bit the Kommandant's exposed wrist and Hans let him go.

"Ow! Little...!" the Kommandant cried, but Martin had already run to the tub.

"*My name is not Martin!*" the boy screamed, desperately trying to dump the chemicals onto the Nazi. The tub, however, was too heavy for Martin, and the Kommandant was easily able to capture him before he could tip anything over. He grabbed the child by his fake blonde hair and yanked him all the way out of Barrack One.

Vilém at first didn't understand what the Kommandant

was doing, but then he realized the Nazi was dragging the howling, thrashing boy to a far-off corner of the Camp. The familiar, terrible stench of soft skin burning became more and more intense, but while Martin gagged and covered his nose, the Kommandant seemed unaffected by the smell.

They arrived at the edge of the Pit. A dancing flame licked the corners of the open-air crematorium. The Kommandant looked down into the Pit and smirked when he saw it was in use. Several new arrivals were being taken care of. The sick. The old. The young. They lay on grates at the bottom, their skin baking, their bodies burning into ash.

Vilém felt ill. He had seen a lot through the eyes of the other victims, but he had never seen what the Nazis did to their bodies. Worse, he felt a sense of satisfaction settle in the Kommandant's chest as he watched the bodies burn, like he was an artist admiring his own completed work.

"I can't breathe..." Martin whimpered, but the Kommandant forced him to look down into the Pit, forced him to stare at his fellow Jews' cremation. It was so hot that the boy's tears evaporated as soon as they left his eyes.

"Look, look boy!" the Kommandant commanded. "Is this where you want to be? You want to be reunited with your mother so badly? Huh? Is that what you want? Is this what you want or do you want to go back to being a good German boy?"

The boy stopped struggling as the Kommandant all but held him directly above the Pit. Martin looked down at the melting, empty eyes of his people. Ashes flew into the air, invading the child's lungs.

"Well? Well? Do you want to go in the Pit, boy? Do you want to be a Jew? Do you want to be a Jew?" the Kommandant snapped. "Am I evil, boy? Am I evil for *stealing* you from this? Go on! You want to go back to the house? Beg me to take you home if this isn't what you want!"

The boy kept his lips tightly pursed to keep the ashes, the taste of death, off his tongue, but he opened his mouth for a mere second to answer: "A German does not beg."

Pride filled the Kommandant's heart, banishing all anger, and he pulled the boy away from the Pit. He let go of the boy's hair and put his hands on his shoulders. Little Martin held his gaze. There wasn't any light in his eyes.

"Good boy," Hans said, patting the child's cheek. "Your mother would have wanted you to be safe. As a German, you will be safe. With me, you will be safe. Just be grateful."

"Okay..." Martin said, still refusing to let his gaze shift, and Vilém could tell that even the Kommandant feared the emptiness in the boy's eyes. Nevertheless, he ignored his own feelings of disquiet and offered the boy his hand.

"Let's go home..." he said. Martin didn't hesitate to cling to the murderer, and as a cloud of ash flew over the two, the memory faded into darkness.

And from there...from there, for some time, he was the perfect German. He didn't question, didn't argue, didn't make a fuss. He did all of his assignments perfectly. He never tried to speak with Pomnenka or any other Jew. When Klaus Heydrich died and I got rid of Fido, he didn't throw a tantrum...he was everything Isaac wasn't.

"He wasn't his own person, he was your puppet," Vilém snapped.

Oh, but not exactly. Under my nose, he associated with the traitor Klammer, he learned Jewish nonsense from the new doctor I got him...and he conspired, conspired to escape. Even when I gave him everything, he still wanted to live as a fugitive Jew.

"You killed his mother. You think for one second he actually wanted to be like you?"

Perhaps I was letting my wants get the best of me. The war was not going well. By the time Klammer pulled off his heist, I knew that everything we had been fighting for, killing for, the great future Heydrich had said I would build...it would never come. Martin was my last chance, my father's last chance, at having a purpose, leaving a mark. I prioritized him above everything those last few weeks before the train was set to leave for Auschwitz.

"Unwrap it, Martin, go on!"

A new memory formed. The Kommandant was sitting cross-legged in the nursery, surrounded by more toys and books than any child could have played with by themselves. A small pile of cards that wished Little Martin a happy birthday, decorated with swastikas and stuffed with Reichsmarks, sat at Martin's side. Martin had unwrapped all but one of his gifts.

"This one's from you?" the child queried, and the Kommandant nodded, grinning so widely that his cheeks hurt. If Vilém had been tossed into this memory with no context, feeling the Kommandant's giddiness and warmth, he would have assumed the child was Gerber's beloved son.

Martin tore the glistening wrapping paper to shreds and pulled out the gift. A smile lit up the boy's face as he hoisted the small machine out of the box. A camera, much smaller than the Kommandant's and clearly brand new.

"And before you ask, I didn't take that from the prisoners," the Kommandant said. "You kept borrowing mine, so I figured you would appreciate it. Do you?"

"Yes! Thank you!" the boy cried, hopping to his feet and wrapping one arm around the Kommandant's neck, giving him a half hug. The Kommandant's heart fluttered and he hesitated to return the embrace. Martin must have never shown him such affection.

"Do you want to take some pictures of your toys?" he asked, and the boy nodded. They spent a few moments posing Martin's stuffed animals and snapping pictures. The Kommandant allowed himself to be silly, letting the boy take pictures of him as he pretended the toys were attacking him.

"Here, sir," the boy said when they had gone through all the toys except one, the little toy cat, whose button eyes had been lovingly replaced. Martin picked it up and tossed it to the Kommandant.

"You can give that away," Martin said. "I'm done with it."

Surprise and joy filled the Kommandant as he looked

from the ratty little toy to the boy who had once loved it so. "Are you sure, Martin?"

"Yes...I don't wanna look at it anymore. It's just a toy anyway," the boy said, lifting up the camera and snapping a picture of the grinning Kommandant. Gerber shoved the little cat into his pocket.

"Come here, you, I'm so proud!" he cried, lifting the boy into the air and spinning him around. Martin seemed surprised and frightened for a moment before he giggled. The Kommandant tossed the child onto the bed.

"Hey, be careful, you may bump me!" the boy cried. "The less I have to see that Jew doctor, the better."

"I'm careful, you know I'm careful!" the Kommandant retorted. "And you won't have to worry about the Jew doctor much longer. I'm looking for a replacement, a proper Aryan replacement. You've earned it, you've earned my trust."

Vilém could feel that announcing this made the Kommandant nervous. No doubt he remembered how Little Martin had reacted the last time he had disposed of a Jewish doctor. But Martin hid his true feelings well and smiled eagerly.

"Good! One less Jew in the house!" the boy declared. "Just don't get rid of my Jew until you find a *really* good Aryan doctor, I don't wanna die!"

Gerber's soul all but burst with happiness at seeing the boy's apparent anti-Semitism. He lovingly patted Martin's head. "I'll get you the best doctor in all the Reich, I promise! It'll be a belated extra birthday present."

"Oh! By the way," the boy cried, hopping to his feet

and pointing to his skull. "I had a birthday request: I don't like that my hair's so curly, it makes me still feel like a Jew. Can we cut it really short so it doesn't curl? Can you use the razor on me?"

"The razor we use for the Jews?" the Kommandant said, grasping a curled strand of the boy's hair. "No, come, I'll trim it for you."

The Kommandant led the boy to his bathroom and pulled his personal razor out of a drawer. Vilém grinned: the Kommandant was unwittingly aiding in the boy's eventual escape.

"Smart kid..." Vilém whispered, but the Kommandant was none the wiser. He looked from the boy to the blade with innocent hesitation.

"Are...you sure?" Hans said, smiling gently. "Have I ever shown you a picture of your father?"

"Isaac Goldstein?" Martin mumbled. Still holding the razor, the Kommandant gestured for the boy to sit on his bed. Hans yanked his old album out of his dresser and opened to the image of him and Isaac as children.

"That's him?" Martin said, prodding the picture with his index finger and staring down at his father's grinning face.

"You look just like him, see? That's how I could tell you were his when I saw you on the Platform."

"I guess..." the boy mumbled, letting his fingers linger just above the faded image. The Kommandant started turning the pages, showing Martin picture after picture until they got to the very back. As he flipped through the album, as the years went on and Isaac grew older and older, Hans began to notice that his not-brother was smiling less and less.

By the time they reached the final image, Isaac was poker-faced. His eyes, once filled with mirth, had become empty.

He looked nothing like the boy in the Christmas picture. But the Kommandant glanced at stony-faced Martin and realized that the last picture of Isaac, the miserable picture...the resemblance was uncanny. If it weren't for the dye and the age difference, they would look identical.

Vilém felt something scratch against the Kommandant's soul. Not exactly realization, and not even close to guilt, but what little wisps of his conscience remained called to him, pointing out what he had done to Isaac, what he was doing to Martin.

Martin pressed his thumb against the solemn Isaac's face. "That's him," he muttered. "That looks like him."

The Kommandant nodded slowly, turning back to the first page, back to the happier Isaac. "You haven't...talked about what he was like to you before..."

"He left when I was little, I've told you that. He was drunk and horrible."

"All the time?" the Kommandant said. "Isaac, he...he had his sins but...he had his good moments."

"The good moments don't matter," Martin declared, shutting the album and shoving it back towards the Kommandant. "Not if everything else is terrible."

"I just...your hair reminds me of him...and..."

"He's the past," Martin proclaimed, grabbing a handful of his curly hair. "The past is gone. It's just sad now. All I wanna do is get to the future. Please, can we cut my hair...Papa?"

Vilém laughed at the boy's deception, and he felt the Kommandant's heart hop with happiness. The Nazi smiled at the new title and placed a hand on the child's shoulder.

"As short as you like!" Hans said. "It will make the dye easier to apply...let's do it!"

He threw the old album aside and took up the razor, cutting the child's hair extra short.

"Nobody will be able to recognize you, Martin," Gerber laughed, and the boy smiled widely.

"I'll thank all the guards for their gifts after the transport leaves tomorrow," Martin said, looking down at the mountain of curly hair that covered the floor and giving it a small nudge with his foot.

"Let's get a picture!" the Kommandant suggested with excitement. The boy posed in front of a swastika flag and shoved his arm into the air, grinning mischievously. The Kommandant, fully convinced that he had won, that the boy was his, snapped a picture.

And the next day...he was gone.

"Pulled one over on ya'!" Vilém laughed. "You didn't *really* think he loved you, did you?"

The spirit said nothing.

"Why would you even want it? A Jew's love?" Vilém inquired. "I thought they were all undesirable."

I thought Martin wasn't.

"Martin never existed, Kommandant!" Vilém snapped. "You tried to turn that little boy into Martin and you failed. And then what?"

And then? Well, of course I tried my best to get him back. I interrogated that traitor Klammer...

Fury and fear like nothing Vilém had ever experienced coursed through the Kommandant as a new memory started with a violent snarl and a kick to Joseph Klammer's face. Klammer was kneeling on the floor of his bare cell, his arms tied behind his back, his face bruised and bloody. Gerber grabbed him by the hair and lifted his head.

"Where did they go?" he demanded, and Klammer spat in his former boss' face.

"Fuck you," Joseph hissed, and the Kommandant, disgusted, threw the young hero to the floor again and kicked him in the stomach, kicked him over and over, his blood pounding in his ears, his heart racing...

And yet even as his bones cracked, even as he was beaten black and blue, Joseph laughed.

"What the *fuck* are you laughing at?" barked the Kommandant. Klammer looked up at Hans and grinned, showing off that the Nazis had knocked out several of his teeth.

"You!" he cried. "The Russians are right at our door about to butcher us and all you care about is killing more Jewish babies!"

"I *care*," the Kommandant insisted, striking Klammer in the gut once more, "that you let the Jews *steal my son!* Tell me where they are and maybe I'll consider letting you die quickly!"

"Your *son*, sure!" Klammer cackled. He sat up slightly, his bright, blazing blue eyes burrowing into the Kommandant's as the bitter mirth drained from his irises.

"I talked to the kid. I talked to him. I know he's not your son. I know you stole him. I don't fucking know why, but you stole him...and he hates you. And he's gonna get away and live a nice long life raised by *Jews!*"

"Enough!" the Kommandant cried, kicking Joseph again, but the Sergeant refused to shut up.

"He's gonna get away, he's gonna be raised by Jews, and he's gonna curse your name forever! Worse! Maybe he'll just forget about you! The Russians will come, the Jews will be free, you'll be dangling from a noose, and all of this misery will be pointless! Your whole life is pointless!"

"ENOUGH! ENOUGH! ENOUGH!"

Hans felt like a bomb had gone off in his chest. He needed to let his anger out. He kicked the prisoner over and over and over...kick, kick, kick...

SMASH!

Until, in the blink of an eye, the memory shifted and in the place of Klammer, the Kommandant brought his boot down on his camera, crushing the machine. He heard a tiny gasp from the snooping Raya Pomnenka, but he ignored it, instead stumbling over to his desk. He grabbed a pack of matches and lit a fire in his trash bin.

Slowly, he started pulling out pictures. Pictures of Martin, smiling with empty eyes, waiting for his escape. Pictures of Martin pretending to be German, pretending to love the Kommandant. He tossed them all into the fire.

He pulled the boy's favorite toy, the little cat, out of his pocket and held it above the flames, but he couldn't bring himself to burn it. The boy had truly loved the cat.

Unlike the pictures that were smoldering in his trash bin, the cat wasn't phony. He set it on his desk, and the little stuffed animal stared at him gloomily as he opened his old leather album.

The pictures of a broken Isaac went first. The Isaac he had poisoned, the Isaac who had lost the hope in his eyes, the Isaac that Martin had known best. They burned first. Slowly, he emptied the albums until only one picture remained: the photo of him and Isaac at Christmas, him and Isaac smiling, him and Isaac as brothers.

He held it above the flames, tears blurring his vision as he dropped it. He watched as the last image of Isaac burned like so many Jews. The ashes flew in his face and the world became gray.

And...well, you know what happened after that. The Russians came and I ended it all. Like Klammer said, it was all pointless.

"So..." Vilém sighed, gripping the family album that still sat on his lap. "You ended it...and then you stayed...because?"

Isn't it obvious? This is my legacy. This failed war, the Camp...this is it. This is all. And I want more. I want to know that my father and I left more than that.

"Through the boy."

He's never come to the Camp. I want to know what became of him. I want...I want for him to have done a great deed, to have become someone of note...I want him to give me meaning. If you can give me that, give me meaning through Martin, I will leave the Camp and move on to whatever's next.

"Right...well, I've got bad news for you. Good news

and bad news." Vilém set the cat on his knee and pressed his palm against the first page of his family album, tapping his finger against the picture of the Svobodas.

"Good news is I don't have to go on a quest. I know exactly what happened to 'Martin.' The boy you stole—his name was Fabian. He's my grandfather."

He peeked through his eyelashes at the picture in front of him, the picture of the grinning, happy Fabian Svoboda, formerly Martin Gerber II, and before that Fabian Goldstein. Vilém had finally recognized his young grandfather on the Platform, but he had bitten his tongue and now...now he could feel the Kommandant's spirit all but explode with surprise and anticipation.

Your grandfather...?

"Fabian befriended my great-uncle Danny. Joseph Klammer was hiding him in your house, right under your nose. Fabian pretended to be a good Nazi to keep you ignorant, to keep Danny safe. When he escaped with the rest of the Jews, my great-grandfather Sam took him in. He raised him as his own."

He...did you know him? Did you know Martin?

"*Fabian.* And I knew him very well. He was an amazing grandfather."

That doesn't matter to me! Did he ever talk about me? Or the war? What became of him? What did he do?

"Absolutely nothing," Vilém declared, his heart swelling with pride. "He kept cactuses. He painted bird-houses with his grandchildren. He was a house painter his whole life. Never stepped foot out of Czechoslovakia. He lived an ordinary life. No grand act of valor, no *point*. He lived, he forgot you, and he had a happy, normal life."

Vilém felt as though a thousand needles were pricking at his flesh as the Kommandant's anger consumed Barrack One.

Then my father died for nothing! I died for nothing!

"No!" snapped Vilém, tucking the toy cat under his arm and standing up. He held his family album like a shield and faced the Kommandant's burning rage. "Everyone in the Camp died for nothing! They died because of stupid, angry people that wouldn't move forward and only dragged their nation back! Fabian lived! Fabian lived a good, happy, gentle life! His life was worth living even if he didn't become a glorious hero or a soldier or whatever twisted creature you wanted to turn him into!"

He only lived because of me!

"You! You! You think everything is about you! But Klammer was right! Your life was pointless! Everything you ever did was pointless! *You* are pointless!"

He dropped the album and stepped forward, gripping the little cat by its neck, and he felt the Kommandant's fury fade into fear.

What are you doing?

"You are nothing! You're a name on a placard that people curse at! Legacy? Meaning? Point? This is your legacy, a legacy of pointless slaughter all done because you wanted everything to fit into a neat little Nazi storybook!"

Enough...

"Well, nothing panned out! You failed at everything! You failed to kill the Jews, you failed Isaac, you even failed to turn Fabian into Martin! And you know what?

I'm getting married, and I'm gonna bring another Jew into the world. Fabian's name will carry on and on, but you? You? The only thing you'll do is *go to Hell!*"

In one swift motion, Vilém tore the toy cat in two. The artifact became nothing but stuffing, fabric, and bad memories, and the Kommandant's worthless soul vanished.

When Vilém opened his eyes, he found himself lying not in the barrack, but in a room drowning in white light. He sat up. He felt weightless; his skin tingled like a current was going through his blood. It was like he had just fallen out of his own body.

He looked to his side and his lips tightened when he saw that the album was gone.

"You can come out now, David!" Vilém cried. He heard the sound of a page flipping and turned around.

There was a boy sitting a few feet away, barely three years old. He was somberly thumbing through the Svoboda family album. He had curly black hair, curly and dark like Sam's, like Fabian's...

The little boy paused as he found one picture of Vilém's grandfather, scowling at Fabian's smiling face. Vilém cleared his throat. The child sighed and looked up, his soft blue eyes meeting the guard's. Despite his apparent age, the child had existed long enough to have gained maturity beyond his appearance. He greeted the Czech man with a crooked smile.

"Hi..." the child muttered. "You did it. Congrats...nephew? Should I call you my nephew?"

"You can call me whatever you want, David," Vilém

said, crawling over to the boy and sitting across from him, offering David Svoboda a comforting smile.

"I get it now," Vilém sighed. "Joseph thought you survived...he thought you were my grandfather. But you...you died in the Ghetto the day before Klammer was reassigned to the Camp. Sam took Fabian in after they met, then they all found Rebecca and...I couldn't tell they weren't related. Fabian looked just like you..."

David nodded, touching the yellow '*Jude*' star that covered his heart. "He did...like an older me."

"How long have you been at the Camp, David?"

"I...move. I'm not like the others. I was never stuck in one place. I just...followed, watched...hoped someone would find out about me. I thought it would be your sister, Emma, the one studying history. But you...you got curious."

"Maybe a little too curious," muttered Vilém. "So...do you have a story to show me?"

"What's there to show?" David snapped, digging his ghostly fingernails into the soft leather of the album. "I got sick, I needed a doctor, I didn't get one...Joseph couldn't do enough. I died...and Mom and Dad replaced me."

The child chuckled ruefully. "Like a goldfish..."

"Or a cactus," Vilém said. "And Danny never even knew."

"He didn't remember me...and Mama and Papa forgot me..." Tears fell from the boy's eyes, dripping onto the album and hissing as they struck the paper, as though the images were an inferno.

"I'm sure they never forgot you, David," Vilém said,

reaching out to the boy. "I saw what Sam was like after you died, he was destroyed. But he had to survive, live, keep Danny safe...and I think he just didn't want to feel sad anymore. He just wanted to keep moving forward..."

"Without me?" whispered David, curling into a little ball. "Because I made them sad."

"Please don't blame yourself, David. I think Fabian and Sam and Rebecca were all afraid of the past. They never talked about it, never got angry about it...but that's not much better than clinging to it like Gerber, hurting yourself and everyone around you to make all the pain worth it. I don't know how they *should* have moved on, but whatever they chose to do, they should have talked about you. You mattered."

"I'm pointless..." the boy said, resting his head on his knees. "I never did anything, never even lived...I just died and made people sad. As soon as they forgot me, they weren't sad anymore."

"David..." muttered Vilém, scooting close to his little great-uncle. He reached out and shut the album, shoving it aside so that nothing sat between him and the ghost.

"Look, I'm not God," he said. "I can't pretend to know how the world works, and I can't pretend to know what went through Sam's mind when he took Fabian in and pretended he was you...but I know that you're not pointless. You don't have to accomplish things or reach a certain age to be a good, worthy human."

"I'm just a number," sobbed David. "One in six million...people will remember Heydrich and the Kommandant...but not me."

"Raya thought the same thing. Was she just a number?"

"No, but *she* lived. Even if you wanna remember me, what's there to remember? I was born, I lived, I got sick, I died..."

"And your papa used to talk about you all the time. And you didn't say 'Papa' for the longest time and Sam was so happy when you finally said it. And when Joseph Klammer saw you...seeing you brought his heart a little closer to changing. You only lived for a few years, David Svoboda, but you changed so many lives, so many little worlds. You know, my grandpa said that Sam and Rebecca, they both passed really quick and really happy. I don't think they ever forgot you...I think they were looking forward to seeing you again. I think they miss you."

David sniffled, wiping his cheeks and gazing up at his great-nephew with wide, worried eyes.

"I'm still mad at them," he hiccupped. "For replacing me...I'm mad at them..."

"You have every right to be mad at them until the end of time, but don't let that anger keep you down here, miserable."

"I'm scared..." David confessed, reaching towards the guard, all semblance of maturity melting away. "What if they still don't wanna see me or think about me?"

"David, I barely know you, and I promise that I will not stop thinking about you. You deserve memory, and you deserve to move on and be happy, and you deserve a big fat apology from your parents...and a big hug too."

Vilém acted without hesitation, grabbing the little

child's hand and gripping it tightly. The child exhaled as though amazed at the sensation of being held, seen, thought of. Slowly, David smiled, and it was a smile so lovely that even if Vilém had tried his hardest, he never would have forgotten it.

"Thanks...Nephew Vilém..." said David. "I'll say hi to Fabian...and Raya and Iveta and everyone else. I'll say hi to everyone."

"You'll be very popular, I'm sure," Vilém chuckled.

"Can you sit...here...with me...just until sunrise?" the boy begged, and Vilém squeezed the lost child's hand.

"Until you're ready," Vilém vowed, and he sat with the boy in the white room until slowly, the light consumed them both.

"Bye, Vilém!" David's little voice called to him, and he felt the child's hand slip away. "Thank you!"

"Vilém...Vilém!"

He felt as though he'd fallen from a two-story building and landed flat on his back. He awoke in Barrack One, covered in stuffing and sweat, blinded by sunlight, gasping for air.

"Jesus, Vilém, you weren't breathing! Are you okay? Don't fucking die in the Camp or I'll never hear the end of it from Ilona!" Alica Doubek's familiar scold alerted him to her presence above him. She helped him sit up, checking his pulse as she did so.

"I'm fine, I'm fine..." Vilém wheezed. "I did it...he's gone...they're all gone now."

"Good...that's good, but...you'll need to be gone...you..." Alica gestured to the remnants of the cat, grimacing as though the sight of artifact-destruction physically pained her.

"I'm sorry...it had to be done," Vilém said.

"I know, Rehor, I know..." Doubek sighed. "But I can't cover for you. You're fired...I'll write you a glowing recommendation and..."

She bit her knuckles and made a noise that sounded like she was choking on an almond. Vilém looked at his boss with concern, worried that she was being possessed, that perhaps the Kommandant hadn't been sent to Hell after all.

"Ms. Doubek..."

"And...you can have a bonus!" she finally gasped, pronouncing the promise in a tone that would have been more appropriate if she were confessing to murder. Vilém couldn't help it: he fell to the barrack floor, laughing.

"Oh, you!" cried Ms. Doubek, giggling and crying all at once. "When will I get a guard like you again?"

"Offer more bonuses!" Vilém joked, grabbing his album and pulling his boss into an embrace. "Bye, Ms. Doubek. You're still invited to the baby shower."

"Damn, thought I'd get out of it..." Doubek grumbled, returning the hug nonetheless. Vilém turned in his uniform, his badge, his flashlight, everything. He even left behind the album so she could use it for the new exhibit.

He left the Camp unemployed, empty-handed...and grinning so widely he drew disapproving glares from the visitors who saw him exit.

Many Years Later:

"Hey, Papa, David got beat up..."

Vilém Rehor stopped doing his homework right away. Normally, an interruption would have aggravated him when he was so wrapped up in finals, but of course his children and their well-being came first. He saved his history assignment and spun his chair around, facing his eldest child.

"How bad?" he asked, and Iveta Rehor, a pretty almost ten-year-old who had inherited her mother's looks, pursed her lips tightly together. It was, unfortunately, practically a rite-of-passage for the Rehor children to be beaten up by anti-Semites at some point in their young lives. Iveta had been beaten up, her younger sister Raya had been beaten up, and now it was the youngest Rehor child's turn to face the ancient hatred.

"Not too bad..." she intoned. "He's not happy, but Uncle Erik was nearby when it happened and beat up the bullies. It was some boys from school, but Erik beat 'em up and took him home."

"Good," Vilém said, rising from his chair. "Where's your mother?"

"Out with Raya. David's down in the shop with Uncle Erik. I put up the 'closed' sign."

"Good girl," Vilém said, patting his daughter's cheek. "I'll take it from here. We'll do our homework together later, okay?"

Iveta, who was the most studious of the Rehor children, smiled and nodded. She and her siblings loved that their father was in university. His status as a part-time student meant that they could all complain about homework together, albeit Vilém, who was pursuing an M.A. in History, certainly had a lot more to complain about regarding his assignments. Still, it was nice. It was something they could relate to.

Vilém sighed as he trudged down the stairs. Experiencing anti-Semitism wasn't something he could relate to. He could never understand what it was like to be his children, to be a minority, to live in the shadow of a genocide and still deal with the fear of it all happening again. He could never understand, but he could always support them, love them, and teach them.

"Hey, man!" Erik greeted him as he arrived down in the shop area. David was sitting at the booth, licking a lollipop and holding an ice pack over a bruised cheek. David looked like Vilém to an almost frightening extent, and even more than that, he looked like Fabian.

"Thanks so much for helping him, dude," Vilém whispered in Erik's ear. "He needs that, to know he has friends who'll defend him."

"I'll fucking deck a Nazi for that kid any day, and I know you would'a done the same for me when we were kids," Erik said with a smirk, patting his friend's shoulder. "Y'know...if all the little mini-Hitlers hadn't been too scared of my grandma to put a hand on me back then."

"Too bad Ilona's gone," muttered Vilém, glancing at a picture of the smiling matriarch that hung on a nearby wall. "If she was still here, she'd murder those little shitheads."

"I'll head up and keep Iveta distracted, you have a father-son whatever," Erik said.

"I'll try my best, but Jana's always better at this kinda thing," Vilém sighed. Erik ran up the stairs and Vilém slowly approached his son, ruffling the seven-year-old's curly hair. The boy looked up and offered Vilém a sparkling smile, a smile that bore a beautiful resemblance to that of his namesake.

"Hey, crazy," Vilém said, sitting beside his son and slowly unwrapping a blob of taffy, molding the candy into a little pyramid. "I heard Erik beat up some dummies."

"It was great!" David said, throwing his ice pack aside and joining his father in playing with taffy like play-dough. "He hit 'em with a plunger and called 'em the s-word."

"Oooh! Well, they earned it...open!" Vilém commanded, plopping his taffy pyramid onto his son's tongue. The boy giggled and the two of them delighted in being mutually gross for a moment.

"Sticky, beep!" David said, poking his father's cheek with a taffy-coated thumb. Vilém snickered and grabbed his son, lifting him onto his lap and squeezing him tenderly.

"You okay?" he asked. David leaned against his father, and Vilém could feel his son tense up.

"Yeah...yeah, Uncle Erik came in, so it's fine..."

"It's okay if it's not fine, son," Vilém said, hugging his child tighter, and he felt the boy settle.

"They said, 'Hitler shoulda' finished you off!' I

dunno what they meant..." David confessed. "Who's Hitler?"

Vilém had been hoping that Jana would be the one to answer that question. She usually was. For Iveta, for Raya...but for David, it was Vilém's turn.

"That's an excellent question, David," he said, resting his chin on the boy's head and smiling as the boy's curly hair tickled his chin.

"This weekend, I'm gonna take you somewhere close by. It's a sad place, and it's a scary place, and it's okay if you cry when we go there. This weekend, you and me, we'll go together, and you can ask any question you want...and...I'll try my best to answer."

THE END

Thank you for reading The Barracks Series!
Elyse Hoffman's next full length novel, *The Book of
Uriel*, is available today! A heartbreaking, enthralling
emotional journey, *The Book of Uriel* is a blend of Jewish
folklore and historical fiction that will enthrall fans of
The Barracks and *The Book Thief*. Order here!
To stay up to date on what will happen next in this
universe and to read similar books, follow Project 613 on
Twitter @Project613Books, on Facebook, and sign up
for updates at Project613Publishing.com! You can also
follow Elyse Hoffman on Goodreads or BookBub or
updates and deals!

Reinhard Heydrich remained by the tower devoted to his killers, his soul seeking out something resembling reality.

Someone approached. Someone clad in black. Black boots stopped in front of him. He winced, and when the figure did not speak right away, he growled.

"Well? Have you made your point? Do you feel better about yourself? Do you, Master?"

www.ingramcontent.com/pod-product-compliance
Lightning Source LLC
Chambersburg PA
CBHW030543130626
46552CB00006B/2397